CAREW

J. C. MILLS

CAREW

KEY PORTER BOOKS

Library and Archives Canada Cataloguing in Publication

Mills, Judith
    Carew / J.C. Mills.

ISBN 1-55263-788-3

    I. Title.
PS8576.I571C37 2006   jC813'.54   C2006-903136-3

The publisher gratefully acknowledges the support of the Canada Council for the Arts and the Ontario Arts Council for its publishing program. We acknowledge the support of the Government of Ontario through the Ontario Media Development Corporation's Ontario Book Initiative.

We acknowledge the financial support of the Government of Canada through the Book Publishing Industry Development Program (BPIDP) for our publishing activities.

Key Porter Books Limited
Six Adelaide Street East, Tenth Floor
Toronto, Ontario
Canada M5C 1H6

www.keyporter.com

Text design and electronic formatting: Martin Gould

Printed and bound in Canada

06 07 08 09 10 5 4 3 2 1

To my dad, with abiding love,
for (among many other wonderful things)
reciting "The Green Eye of the Yellow God"
when I was small—a little seed of imagination.

There's a one-eyed yellow idol to the north of Khatmandu,
There's a little marble cross below the town;
There's a broken-hearted woman tends the grave of Mad
    Carew,
And the Yellow God forever gazes down.

—from "The Green Eye of the Yellow God," by J. Milton Hayes

PROLOGUE

IN NORTHERN NEPAL, not far from the fabled city of Kathmandu, lie the deep, lush forests of the Langtang valley. Nestled in the shadow of Mount Everest—the earth's highest peak—is a place rich in legend. Until just a few decades ago, Langtang was a fortress, shielded from the prying eyes of the modern world by a long line of reclusive rulers, their protective habits fuelled by centuries of political turmoil and a wariness of western ways. But even now, as foreigners slip across man-made borders to conquer and explore the peaks and valleys and deep river gorges of Nepal, the country struggles to remain as it always has been: a land cloaked in myth and mystery.

Deep within Langtang, in sprawling tangles of old-growth trees, the air hangs thick with the intoxicating scent of delicate orchid, of iris, of blue gentian and primrose; aromas that seem to grow still sweeter whenever the summer monsoon rains descend. There is an abundance of birdlife in the sanctuary of the forest, most noticeable to those who possess considerable patience. Many who live here among the oak, hemlock, juniper and chir pine can be shy and elusive. The cuckoo and barbet, rosefinch and whistling thrush, might tease with a note or two of their distinctive songs before escaping into the dark, leafy shadows like thieves in the night. Other inhabitants abound in the deep recesses of the valley, too: shimmering snakes and butterflies, snow leopards, wild dogs and red pandas, timid musk deer, Himalayan black bears, graceful langur monkeys and the slow, waddling pikas. All live out the natural patterns of their lives, oblivious to the teeming world of modern humankind and all that it has created—science and finance, technology and warfare.

Despite its remoteness from the modern world—or perhaps because of it—the valley is a place where people with dreams of adventure and glory routinely gather on their journeys northward: to scale the loftiest peaks on the planet, to uncover the legendary kingdom of Shangri-La, or perhaps to trail a yeti, mythical snow beast of the Himalayas. Those with a hunger of the spirit also have their pilgrimages: to the birthplace of Siddhartha Gautama, the disillusioned prince who would become the great Lord Buddha, or to the crest of the cloud-shrouded mountains and holy lakes of Gosainkunda, divine home to the gods and goddesses of the Hindu faith and the shrines of Shiva.

But this place is not always a welcoming host. Even those with the best of intentions have admitted to feeling like intruders here. Many visitors, especially those who seek the thrill of conquest or the inspiring vistas of the higher altitudes, report that they have experienced mystical visions, as if they were drifting in and out of a dream. To some these visions bring heightened awareness and a sense of euphoria. But it is sometimes described, too, as a feeling that can abruptly change, transforming from a state of well-being into one that is hostile and menacing, as if something—or someone—were trying to push them away. A few have even spoken to friends and colleagues of strange and foreboding premonitions, only to perish hours later, swiftly and silently, under an avalanche of tumbling mountain snow.

Because of its spiritual richness, large areas of the Langtang valley have been decreed sacred—a home to living deities, a place where no animal may be killed, and where no man should interfere with the natural cycle of life and death and rebirth. And so, for year upon year, this delicate balance, this intricate dance of earthly existence, of young and old, male and female, sun and moon, flesh and spirit, has been playing out in the great shadow of the Himalayas, the "abode of the gods." And all the while, the rest of the "civilized" world, with all its thoughtlessness and waste, avarice and cruelty, creeps closer and closer....

1

THE CAPTURE

THWACK!

The long switch of maple wood slapped against the side of the cage like a crack of thunder. Caught by surprise, the Creature let out a shrill cry, pulled his slender hand back into the safety of the shadows and began to tremble. He should never have reached for the bars. It had been instinct—an attempt to steady himself when one of the porters, stumbling on the rain-soaked path, allowed the cage to swing too close to the ground.

They had been travelling for many hours in the steadily falling rain, following an old forest trail, before he had summoned enough courage to slink forward into the light. He had been desperate to look out by then, to spot anything he might know—a familiar thicket of trees, a particular clearing or a friendly flock of birds—but his curiosity had been rewarded with such numbing pain that he instantly regretted his actions.

The edge of the metal enclosure collided with a thick puddle of mud, sending a spray of foul-smelling brown ooze onto his body. Cold and startled, the Creature retreated into the far corner of the enclosure, rubbing his bleeding knuckle. He listened as an angry screech echoed through the trees.

Sounds like this were not unfamiliar. The Creature had heard them before; more and more often, in fact, over the last few years. The noises—screams and yelps and cackles and low, quiet murmuring—came from the Strange Ones that walked on two legs. Their peculiar shouts and bellows had occasionally drifted up to his perch at the top of the forest canopy. But this time was different. He had never been this close to them before and though he did not fully understand the meaning, the sounds they were making seemed much more menacing than he remembered. He wished he had not ventured out at all that morning, but he had awoken with an appetite for walnuts; the sweet, dark, succulent ones that grew further down the forested slopes, where little streams of bubbling water, ice cold and sparkling, danced across the rocks. Silently, he had descended from the safety of the high branches and down the slippery valley walls. Lost in the enjoyment of his breakfast feast, he had not sensed them as they crept up behind him—not until it was too late. He had struggled valiantly to escape, but the Strange Ones held the advantage of surprise, and a far greater strength than he could overcome.

The angry voice tore through the forest again. Wincing in pain and fear, the Creature shuffled as far back into the darkness as he could, pressing his spine against the end of the cage where an old piece of thick, black oilcloth had been draped over the bars. He had no intention of creeping up to the front again, to the place where shafts of daylight were spilling through onto the cage floor, no matter how tempting it might be. He had learned that lesson well enough.

The rain continued to fall, playing its sad song on the oil-cloth roof of the Creature's enclosure. As the hours passed and the rain showed no sign of abating, the aching in his knuckle slowly began to subside. In its place, an altogether different kind of discomfort started to grow. It was all-consuming, not so much a physical sensation as a feeling of overwhelming despair. It worsened—radiating out to every fibre of his being—whenever he allowed himself to think of the Other. The One left behind, the One they had not seen.

As the cage continued to rock to and fro, the Creature glanced down at himself and gasped in horror. The beautiful fur that covered his body, the soft, golden strands that used to shimmer in the light (the very same ones that the Other had so lovingly stroked and groomed) had become matted and dull. He sniffed the air and closed his eyes in disgust. He smelled now of rancid mud. For a moment, he was thankful that she could not see him. He tried in vain to smooth out his coat with the long, thin fingers of his uninjured hand. As he did, a few strands came loose and drifted down onto the cold, wet floor of the cage. He opened his mouth to cry out, but quickly stopped himself, deciding to hold his anguish inside instead. It might not be wise, he thought, to attract any more attention. Sighing, the Creature curled his long, golden tail around his toes to provide some comfort. It was no use. His heart was as heavy as a stone. He closed his emerald eyes— eyes that had once been so deep and glowing, eyes that in all the centuries of his existence had never lost their fire before. Not once. Not ever. Not until now.

"Are you idiots deaf or just thick? Haven't I warned you about this?" The scream sliced through the air, and although the Creature could not determine the meaning of the words, he knew that anger and hatred lay in the heart of the Strange One who uttered them. All at once, the swaying motion he had been bracing his body against for the last several hours stopped. He lurched forward, eyes wide open, limbs scraping painfully against the cold metal bars of the cage. The screeching one—the Angry One—was standing very close now. As he steadied himself again, the Creature could feel the heat of his rage filtering through the layer of dark, draped cloth. His green eyes darted back and forth, searching for the tiny tear in the fabric he had noticed earlier. He was curious. What did this Angry One look like, this one whose voice oozed with such hatred? There it was! A thin track of light trickled onto the cage floor. The Creature carefully positioned one green eye against the tear and slowly pulled the edges of the fabric apart.

There were several other Strange Ones in the group outside, and they were grumbling unhappily, heads down, feet kicking at the muddy earth. The Angry One was not hard to spot. As the Creature watched, he strode toward the group, waving his arms. He grabbed the switch of maple wood from the hands of another—a taller, larger being—and swiftly cracked it in two across his knee. Snarling, he stormed to the front end of the enclosure and bent down. His pushed his face, bright red and twisted with anger, right up against the cage door.

The Creature wriggled backward as fast as he could as a piece of snapped branch snaked toward him through the bars. He braced himself and turned his head, holding all of his muscles as tight as he could, waiting for the sharp end of the stick to poke him. Nothing. A moment passed, then another. Finally, the Angry One removed his weapon. He stood up and spat a big ball of saliva onto the ground. He threw the broken branch down, kicking it aside with the toe of his boot.

"Look at it!" The Angry One was shouting again, and the others glanced up sullenly at his words, their faces pale and strained, their voices suddenly silent. "A capture like this could lead to some nice bonuses for you clods, but not if it's beaten up! We could all be fired on the spot for this!"

For a moment, none of the Strange Ones moved. Then, finally, one dared to speak. The Creature winced at the sound of his voice. It was the Large One; the man who had struck him earlier.

"Ah, come on now, boss." The Large One's voice was softer than the others', but it was menacing just the same. The Creature leaned forward, struggling to understand what was happening. "It's just a stupid beast! And besides, it was staring at me with those freaky green eyes and flexing its nasty little claws. We have a right to protect ourselves, Darby!"

The Angry One—Darby?—seemed enraged by the Large One's words. "That's Mr. Darby to you, Tyrone," he shouted, spinning sideways to face the others. "It's Mr. Darby to all of you!" He braced his legs far apart, standing firm on the spot, and stared them down one by one, until each had dropped his eyes to the ground. And then, strangely, he began to smile—a weird, white, toothy grin that sent an icy shiver up the Creature's spine.

Turning away from the group, The Angry One once again made his way to the cage, squatting down in the mud and pressing his face against the bars. "You idiot! It's barely the size of a housecat!" He began to snicker, poking the end of his pale pink tongue in and out. "Here kitty, kitty, kitty," he said. The lilting tone of his voice did little to disguise the cruelty of his words. The Creature lowered his head. He did not want to look at this horrible being any longer.

The Strange Ones, still standing awkwardly in their group, began chuckling nervously. Suddenly, however, the snickering stopped. Slowly, the Creature opened his eyes. The expression on the Angry One's face had soured again. He was staring straight ahead, eyes burning wild, at the thick crust of drying blood on the Creature's knuckle. He rose up again, screaming even louder now at the Large One, his voice bubbling up into a shriek. "Did you draw blood with that wretched stick, Tyrone? Did you?" It was a sound so harsh, so hateful, that the Creature flinched and tightened his muscles again, slowly turning his head toward the oilcloth. He could still see the Large One, trembling a little now, through the small slit.

The Angry One took a deep breath, then slowly exhaled, his eyes flashing with rage—deep, dark, sparkling orbs, as black as the thick curls of hair that framed his head. "At a loss for words, are you? Well, that's a switch." He glared long and hard at the Large One, then shifted his gaze to include the others in the group. A thin smile began to spread across his lips. "Now don't any of you start thinking I've gone soft," he continued, his voice more subdued now. "If you're going to discipline these rotten little beasts, you have to learn to hit them in a place that doesn't show—a nice, fur-covered backside, perhaps? Isn't that right, Tyrone?"

Tyrone nodded. He looked at the rest of the group and chuckled, relieved, no doubt, that the Angry One seemed to have calmed down. In his enclosure, the Creature braced himself. The energy in the air hadn't changed; the Angry One was still seething with rage, and it was about to boil over. The shriek came suddenly, sending the few birds that remained in the area into the sky and causing the startled Strange Ones to cringe and huddle closer together. "But if you EVER think of drawing blood like that again, Tyrone, you are OUT! OUT! DO YOU HEAR ME?" The Angry One lunged toward Tyrone, bellowing the last few words directly into the man's face. "I'll personally see to it that you're on the next flight out of here, and I'll make sure you never work in this field again! Am I making myself clear?" As he spoke, the man named Darby slowly reached down and pulled a large, ivory-handled hunting knife from the rim of his boot. He slipped the blade out of its leather sheath and carefully ran his fingers along the sharp, gleaming edge, all the while fixing his steel-cold eyes on Tyrone's frightened face.

The Large One began to whimper. His eyes darted back and forth, looking for help, as beads of sweat trickled down his forehead. His voice, when he spoke, was unsteady, and the Creature could barely make out the sounds. "Yes, sir. Perfectly clear ... sir."

Without warning, Darby shot forward with the knife, pressing it against Tyrone's beefy neck. He gasped, his face turning ashen as he struggled to hold still. With his other hand, Darby fumbled in his pocket for a match, struck it hard against his pant leg and pushed the flaming stick forward. Behind the oilcloth, the Creature's eyes grew wider. When it looked as if Tyrone was about to collapse, Darby grinned and quickly pulled the weapon and the spent match away. A slimy black leech squirmed on the tip of the knife blade.

Tyrone blew the air out of his lungs and shuddered.

"Nasty little things, aren't they?" Grinning, Darby leaned forward and whispered his words into Tyrone's ear. A thin drop of blood trickled from the spot on his neck where the leech had been sucking. He wiped the wetness away and nodded nervously. Darby flicked the still wriggling leech off the knife and onto the ground, then crushed it flat against the wet earth with the heavy heel of his boot.

The Creature trembled and lowered his eyes. When he glanced up again, Darby was resheathing the blade. He quickly popped the weapon back into his boot top and strolled to the edge of the forest path where an old alder tree had fallen. He straddled the thick trunk, flicked off a couple of leeches, then slowly laid his lean body down its length, crossing his boots at one end and folding his hands behind the back of his head at the other. The rain had finally moved off and bright rays of afternoon sun filtered through the trees and played across his face. It must have felt wonderfully warm, the Creature imagined, as he rocked himself back and forth in the cage, wet and shivering.

Darby let out a deep and satisfied sigh, then bent his knee and loudly tapped the heel of his boot against the tree bark. When he spoke again, his voice was almost friendly. "I believe I might enjoy a little personal service today," he said. "Tyrone, bring me my sandwich and tea, and make it fast." The Creature turned his head to see Tyrone scurry over to one of the cage bearers. He stopped beside a huge sack and pulled out a green flask and a small paper-wrapped bundle.

While Tyrone fumbled noisily with the paper packaging, unwrapping the first food the Creature had smelled since his interrupted breakfast, Darby turned his face back toward the warmth of the sun. He shut his eyes and sighed again. For a moment, the forest was quiet. The Creature was tired. This journey had been long and uncomfortable. He was cold and hungry, and he wanted nothing more than to slip through the bars and make his way back to the Other. He opened his eyes and peered out of his cage once more. Would he even be able to find her now?

The Creature's thoughts were interrupted, once again, by Darby's shouting. "Mister Tyrone, is there some reason that I'm still waiting for my lunch?" His voice shot through the thick, steamy air as he slowly shifted his body down the tree trunk, searching, it appeared, for a flatter section of bark to rest his back against. He raised one arm high above his head, making a tight fist over and over with his hand, flexing all of his sinewy muscles. When he tired of that, he let the other hand dangle to the ground, slowly moving it through the dirt until the tips of his fingers made contact with a rock, the size of an egg. He turned his head toward the Creature's cage. With one powerful swing of his arm, Darby let the rock fly. It hit the cage with enough force to send it teetering back and forth on its metal base. Inside, the Creature toppled backward, jarring his spine against the bars. Forgetting for a moment about his injury, he reached his thin arm forward, allowing his hand to fall hard and flat against the metal floor. He winced in pain and let out a pitiful little cry. Where was Tyrone? Perhaps the food he was preparing would improve Darby's mood.

Finally! As the Creature watched, hunger gnawing at his stomach, Tyrone made his way across the clearing with a lumpy, wilting bundle clutched in one hand, and a shiny container in the other. "It's about time!" Darby reached out his hand as he spoke, snatching the food and drink away.

especially now that she was accompanying her uncle on more of his expeditions abroad, but her hair was the one personal feature that linked her with her mother. Rosalie Parnell had had the same raven-coloured locks as her daughter—long and curled and a little unruly—and whenever Lucy looked at the tiny photograph of her mother in the silver locket she wore around her neck, it gave her some comfort to imagine how much more alike they might have been.

"Just a second," she called out, pulling the blanket off her legs and swinging them sideways and down to the floor. "I'll be right there."

Still groggy from her dream, Lucy stumbled a little as she hastily knotted the ties of her bathrobe and reached for the doorknob. She winced as the rusty hinges squealed against the door frame, forgetting for a moment that there were no other guests in the hotel to disturb. Shortly after their arrival, Lucy had learned that the monsoon season, with its abundance of mudslides and leeches, was not the most popular time for trekking in Nepal. As the locals she had befriended often told her, "leeches come, tourists go."

"Come in," Lucy said, stepping aside as Sir Jeffrey hobbled past and into the small room. He stopped and leaned toward her, putting all of his weight onto the walking stick in his hand. His eyes twinkled with excitement. "What is it?" she asked, still rubbing the sleep from her eyes. "What's going on?"

"An unusual animal has been discovered, my dear! Can you believe it? Finally!" Sir Jeffrey crowed with delight. "It's alive and well, I'm happy to report—and it appears to be something quite unique, if what Mr. Darby tells me is accurate."

Lucy's throat suddenly felt dry. "He actually found one *alive*? A ... a yeti?" She held her breath.

"Oh goodness, no," her uncle replied, shaking his head.

Lucy slowly breathed out again. "Oh."

"From what I've heard so far, though, it may end up being quite a significant find," Sir Jeffrey responded, sensing Lucy's disappointment. "Apparently, it's a small fur-bearing creature, possessing a number of rather surprising features—scales and feathers and such. Most remarkable! We won't know what we have for sure, of course, until I've had the opportunity to examine it."

"How did they find it?" asked Lucy.

"Quite by accident, I understand," Sir Jeffrey responded. "As Mr. Darby explained it, they were up beyond the snow line, at the Tibetan border. They had just finished interviewing a young Sherpa boy about the alleged yeti prints he'd spotted some days earlier. It turned out, however, to be nothing more than the hoof marks of a very large yak that had taken to wandering away from one of the village pens during the night. Our men were understandably disappointed by the news, especially when Mr. Darby decided to terminate the expedition then and there. I imagine he made the right decision, though. They had been trekking for three weeks and two of the group were already displaying some early signs of altitude sickness—shortness of breath, headache, nausea, that sort of thing. They had barely started their descent when they literally fell upon this odd creature."

"Just like that?" Lucy asked, making a face.

Something wasn't sitting right. And the fact that Francis Darby was at the centre of the story only heightened Lucy's suspicions. She couldn't believe she had once found the man attractive! The fact that he wasn't *that* much older than her-self—only seven years or so—had made her daydreams seem almost reasonable at first. It had all been silly nonsense, an infatuation brought on by his dark, brooding looks and the sultry Irish lilt in his voice. It didn't take long for Lucy to dis-cover another side of Darby, one that she found quite disturbing. Maybe it was the way he had taken to looking at her lately—a glance that landed somewhere between a smirk and a leer. Maybe it was something else—a "sixth sense." Whatever the reason, Lucy didn't trust Francis Darby. Not one bit.

Sir Jeffrey, oblivious to his niece's concerns, seemed happy enough with Darby's performance. Based on his impressive credentials, he had offered Darby the job of field assistant. And now it was too late for Lucy to do anything about it. Besides, she was far too embarrassed to air her per-sonal feelings about Darby with her uncle or anyone else.

"A rare stroke of luck finding something up there, wouldn't you say?" Sir Jeffrey continued.

"What's that?" Lucy muttered absently, her mind still swirling with thoughts of Francis Darby.

"The elevations, my dear! You know how inhospitable the high Himalayas can be." He rubbed his hands together with anticipation. "I'm anxious to understand how this little creature manages to survive! It must have a hardy constitu-tion—or a hide as tough as a yak's, at the very least!"

"Wouldn't it have been better if they'd tried to observe it first?" Lucy asked. "They could have taken photographs, then mapped an exact location so that *you* could have returned and assessed things before making a live capture."

"In a perfect world, perhaps," Sir Jeffrey sighed. "But Mr.

Darby tells me that the field cameras jammed."

"Both of them?"

"Perhaps it was the cold air. Or the altitude." Sir Jeffrey glanced down at his bandaged foot. "It doesn't really matter, I suppose. Look at me! I'm in no position to mount a second expedition right now, anyway...."

"I don't know," Lucy interrupted. "I just have this feeling that maybe they should have ..."

"I'm afraid it's too late to second-guess Mr. Darby, my dear," Sir Jeffrey replied. "He made a professional assessment up there and decided to bring the specimen *here* for study. We'll just have to respect that. Of course, we'll be extremely careful with the beast and return it to the high country as soon as we're able. In any event, we'll have to be patient until morning. Mr. Darby tells me it was an exhausting trek down the mountains. He's very wisely elected to let the men rest where they are until first light. In the meantime, I've put a call in to the Wildlife Society's London office. They're going to send out their best wildlife photographer as soon as possible. He's probably already on his way. I agree, of course, that it would have been better if the men could have documented everything at their end at the actual moment of discovery, but these things don't always go as planned." Sir Jeffrey sighed. "And we've not been blessed with the best of luck lately, have we?"

Lucy grabbed her uncle by the arm as the walking stick in his hand suddenly began to wobble.

"Blasted foot!" he snapped to himself. "And it couldn't have come at as worse time, either! This might be a very significant discovery, Lucy! Just imagine! Perhaps they've stumbled onto something akin to the okapi. That fellow certainly caused quite a stir when he was discovered back in 1901. Or it could be as monumental as finding the coelacanth. We believed he'd been extinct for the last sixty-four million years until he landed in some fisherman's net! Or the giant Vietnamese barking deer or the Vu Quang ox ... or the Komodo dragon, or ..."

Sir Jeffrey suddenly stopped speaking. He grimaced in pain as he glanced down at his bulbous right foot, looking, in its currently bandaged state, like a great white balloon. He gave it a gentle tap with the end of his stick and sighed again.

"And I would have been right there to see it all, too, Lucy, if it hadn't been for this damnable gout!" he lamented. "It wasn't as if I'd been neglecting my medications, you know. I've been following those instructions on the bottle to the letter. I'm at a loss to explain it." He looked up at his niece with an expression of regret. "Perhaps you should have gone with Mr. Darby, so at least one of us could have been there to see!"

"No!" The thought of being trapped in the wilderness with Francis Darby was intensely distressing to Lucy. Quickly calming herself, she continued. "That would have been selfish of me, Uncle Jeff. You needed me here. Just look at your foot! Besides, I'm sure Mr. Darby was able to handle everything quite capably at his end. You said so yourself."

Even as the last few words were spilling from her lips, Lucy was already having trouble believing them. She led Sir Jeffrey to the far side of the room and helped him to an overstuffed chair that sat in one corner. He eased himself down into it with some difficulty, then looked up at her and smiled.

"I really don't know what I'd do without you, my dear. These last few weeks would have been absolutely unbearable without your pleasant company."

Lucy smiled back. Sir Jeffrey Parnell was a likeable man, rarely prone to moods or melancholy, and even though he did have an annoying tendency to be forgetful and vague at times, Lucy adored him. Just three years old when her parents were killed in an automobile crash, Lucy had been placed under the guardianship of Sir Jeffrey, her father's much older brother and her only remaining relative. He was a confirmed bachelor back then, with no family of his own. His principal interest in life was to spend as much time as he could manage in the stuffy specimen rooms at the British Museum in London, recataloguing the aging collection of animal pelts and bird bodies that resided there. Now that she was older, Lucy imagined it must have come as a great shock to poor Sir Jeffrey to suddenly have his quiet, sterile world invaded by an active and demanding three-year-old, and to have the well-being of a living "human" creature to consider. But not once, in all the thirteen years she had been with him, had she ever had reason to question his love or devotion. She especially loved the days he allowed her to escort him to the museum. It was during many hours of wandering through the miles of exhibits there that she had developed a passionate appreciation for the natural world, and an understanding of the importance of her uncle's work. It was at the museum, too, that she had made an important choice. Just weeks away from the milestone of her sixteenth birthday, Lucy Parnell had decided to follow in her uncle's footsteps and dedicate her life to science.

"Can I get you anything, Uncle Jeff?" Lucy asked, hovering over him.

"No, my dear. I'm quite alright."

"Then you really should try and get some rest before Mr. Darby arrives with the animal."

Sir Jeffrey sighed and nodded his head, but Lucy was not convinced. He was like a child just now, she thought, waiting for a visit from Santa Claus. Not that she couldn't understand his eagerness.

Over the last few years Sir Jeffrey's interests had taken a distinctly different path than the one followed by more traditional zoologists. He had begun to study cryptozoology and had developed quite a passion for his new pursuit. Cryptozoology owed its origins to many dedicated academics. Most notable among its founders was Dr. Bernard Heuvelmans, a respected Belgian biologist who brought the term to life, from the Greek word *kryptos*, meaning secret, hidden and unknown. It was a field that had managed, in just a few decades, to attract an expanding list of highly regarded scientists—Sir Jeffrey Parnell among them. It was *their* sincere desire to find and preserve the world's lost and undiscovered animals that was now inspiring the hearts and minds of many other dedicated men and women. But there was another side to the cryptozoology coin: a side that leaned toward the strange, the bizarre, even the supernatural. This was the quest for creatures with glowing eyes—those "cryptids" that appeared to exist only in tribal myths or the excited ramblings of a handful of people who claimed to have seen them. Despite the lack of evidence, it was this branch of the science that was attracting and fascinating a whole contingent of New Age oddballs and enthusiastic amateurs.

On rare occasions throughout the years, Sir Jeffrey would obtain enough funding to mount an expedition to a remote area of the world, especially following a reported sighting of a new species or the sudden appearance of a long-believed extinct one. If any of these trips happened to fall during a school break, Lucy would plead with her uncle to be taken along. Due to the very generous financial support of a new and mysterious benefactor, Lucy had managed to join several expeditions in just the last few months. The first was to Inverness, Scotland, home of the Loch Ness Monster. Another took them to the Congo, where the elusive "Mokele-mbembe"—a dinosaur-like creature and possible survivor from the prehistoric age—was said to lurk. Finally, there had been a short junket to British Columbia, where not one, but two legendary creatures purportedly roamed: Ogopogo, serpent monster of Lake Okanagan, and Sasquatch, a gigantic hairy ape-man and northern cousin to one of the most famous cryptids of all: Bigfoot. And now they were in Nepal, home to the mythical yeti—the "Abominable Snowman" of modern -day culture.

Lucy knew that her uncle was a little embarrassed by these trips. His own cryptozoological interests were not quite as "headline-grabbing" as his mysterious financier's. Nevertheless, it didn't seem appropriate to kick a gift horse with that kind of money in the mouth, even if the man was adamant that his donations be spent on searching for the more famous "cryptids"—loch monsters and sasquatches, ship-devouring sea creatures, flying mothmen, giant phantom panthers, even the hideous, blood-sucking, chupacabra monsters of Mexico. Still, it was Sir Jeffrey's sincere hope that while they were out searching for these "bigger fish"— which he personally doubted they would ever find—he might stumble upon an unassuming, previously undiscovered miniature tree frog in deepest Africa, or a flock of Carolina parakeets that had taken a migratory "wrong turn" and wound up in the wilds of the Pacific Northwest. These encounters weren't totally unheard of. After all, just a few months ago, the great ivory-billed woodpecker had been "rediscovered" in a swamp in the southern United States. It may not have seemed like much to most people, but a discovery like that would have been the ultimate achievement for a dedicated scientist and environmentalist like Sir Jeffrey Parnell. Of course, Lucy would have loved nothing better than to see her uncle enjoy the quiet sort of discovery he craved. Secretly, though, she hoped that they might find something a bit more romantic and exciting—a small yeti, perhaps—just once.

Lucy helped her uncle settle into the chair, laying a blanket across his legs. Next to him, a tiny window, framed on either side with strips of faded blue cloth, looked out onto the centre of Dhunche, a small village that served as the hub for the surrounding region. This motley collection of narrow streets and stone buildings had not been their intended destination. But the gruelling eight-hour trip north from Kathmandu, on roads that would have been judged impassable by most western standards, was as much as Sir Jeffrey and his painfully throbbing toes could endure. Going any further, especially since much of the remaining trip to the high country was to continue on foot, was simply out of the question. Lucy and her uncle took refuge at the most hospitable-looking hotel in the village, a drab but relatively clean establishment. After much discussion, Sir Jeffrey reluctantly agreed to allow the expedition—led by Francis Darby—to proceed without him.

Lucy glanced down at her watch. It was already ten minutes past midnight. Turning to the window, she pushed one of the blue strips of cloth that served as a curtain aside and peered into the night sky through the thick pane of rippled glass. After weeks of incarceration here, Lucy had grown more familiar with the scene below than she cared to admit. There was little movement on the street now, apart from the scruffy trio of mongrel dogs that always seemed to be prowling about in search of dinner scraps. She turned around and looked at her uncle.

"Are you sure you don't want anything?" Lucy offered, stifling a yawn. "A cup of *chiyaa* tea, perhaps?"

Sir Jeffrey looked up at his niece and grinned. "Well, that *is* a tempting proposition," he replied, then quickly added, "With an extra dollop of that delightful condensed milk ... and a couple of pieces of buttered toast, too, please. If it's not any trouble, of course."

Lucy smiled at him and shrugged her shoulders. "I doubt the kitchen's still serving anything but boiled tea water at this time of night, but I'll see what I can do."

Lucy was halfway out the door before something compelled her to walk back to the window. She lifted an edge of the ragged curtain with the tip of her finger. Something had seemed different when she'd looked out before, something she couldn't quite put her finger on. Looking again, nothing appeared to be out of the ordinary. The air was quiet and still. Perhaps it was just the strange glow the moon was casting on the passing clouds that had attracted her attention. Whatever the cause, the atmosphere outside seemed strangely unnatural. All at once, Lucy felt an overpowering sense of dread, as if something, somewhere, was terribly wrong. As her fingers instinctively wandered to the silver locket and chain that hung from her neck, the eerie howl of a jackal shattered the night's silence, rushing through her like a jolt of electricity. Pressing her face against the windowpane, Lucy stared straight down to the street below. The three scavenging village dogs had stopped dead in their tracks—frozen mid-stride, as if waiting for something else to happen. When the jackal howled for a second time, all three sat down on their haunches; when a third and final howl pierced the air, they threw back their heads and let out a cry so mournful and so sad that it filled Lucy's heart with an inexplicable sorrow.

3

THE RETURN

THE SUN WAS ALREADY trickling through the room's thin curtains when Francis Darby arrived back in town. Sir Jeffrey, still propped up in the big chair by the window and still clutching his walking stick, was sleeping peacefully, having finally succumbed to exhaustion in the early hours of the morning. Lucy, curled up on the edge of her bed, dozed more fitfully than her uncle. She was the first to hear the knock at the door. She slipped off the bed, retied her bathrobe as tight as she could around her waist and gave Sir Jeffrey a nudge in his side.

"Be right there!" she called out. "Come on, Uncle Jeff," she whispered into her uncle's ear. "Please wake up! I think Mr. Darby is here!"

Not relishing the thought of opening the door to Darby all by herself, especially in her night clothes, Lucy tugged forcefully on the sleeve of her uncle's jacket until he started to awaken. Sir Jeffrey snorted loudly a couple of times as Lucy repositioned the walking stick in his hand, helped him to his feet and pushed him forward to the door. Reaching around his rather large waist, she slipped the bolt out of the lock with one hand and turned the knob with the other. She stood back and waited.

"Ahhh … there you are Mr. Darby!" Sir Jeffrey stifled a yawn as the door slowly swung open. He placed one hand on Francis Darby's shoulder and gave it a firm but friendly squeeze.

There was an awkward moment of silence as the three of them stared at each other. Lucy could feel Darby's eyes burning into her. He seemed disappointed, frustrated. Had he expected to find her alone? Feeling the blood rushing to her cheeks, she took a deep breath and folded her arms protectively across her body.

"Well?" Sir Jeffrey finally blurted out. "Where is it?"

Darby smiled. "Haven't you heard, Sir Jeffrey," he replied, as he continued to stare at Lucy, "that patience is a virtue?"

"Patience, Mr. Darby?" Sir Jeffrey replied. "This is hardly a time for patience! Have you brought the animal with you or not?"

"Well, of course I have," he sighed. "But we're all very tired, you know. It only seemed fair to give the men some time to get themselves cleaned up. I can't tell you how long I've been wanting a nice soothing bath."

Had Darby just winked at her? Lucy glanced across to her uncle but he hadn't seemed to notice.

"Don't worry yourself about it, Sir Jeffrey," Darby continued. "I'll be bringing the beast up to you soon enough."

"But Mr. Darby! I really must insist that I see it immediately. I—"

Sir Jeffrey's words were interrupted by the arrival of a

small, middle-aged Nepali man. He stood on the landing out-side Lucy's door, half-hidden by Darby's bulkier body.

"Yes, Tenzing, what is it?"

"Phone, Mr. Jeffrey. Downstairs. Come now. Man say very important." The hotelier was grinning and nodding his head vigorously.

"Who in the blazes could that be?" Sir Jeffrey snapped, as he struggled through the narrow doorway, pushing his walk-ing stick ahead of him. Lucy took his arm and helped him into the hall.

"I suppose you might as well have that bath now, Mr. Darby!" Sir Jeffrey shouted, as Lucy led him down the stairs. "But after I've taken this call, I'll need to examine the ani-mal. Is that understood?"

Lucy glanced over her shoulder, curious to see Darby's reaction to her uncle's stern tone.

"Whatever you say."

Darby's words were accompanied by a casual shrug of his shoulders, but Lucy could sense that he was irritated by something; even a little nervous. He lingered in the hallway, looking as if he wanted to follow them. What was he up to? Lucy gave him her best glare and continued down the stairs. When she looked again, he was gone.

Ten minutes later, Lucy was once again on the stairs. The phone call had thrown Sir Jeffrey into such a tizzy that Lucy was forced to hold onto him quite tightly, just to keep him from stumbling.

"I never imagined, Lucy, not even in my wildest dreams," Sir Jeffrey babbled. "Melville Carew! Who would have guessed that our mysterious benefactor would turn out to be a man of such international notoriety! And one of the world's richest, too! And to think! He wants to visit us on one of our expeditions! It's all rather sudden, isn't it? Goodness, my dear! We don't have much time to prepare, do we?"

"When did Mr. Carew say he'd be here?" Lucy asked, struggling to follow her uncle's jumbled thoughts.

"Sometime tomorrow," he replied excitedly.

They had reached the top of the stairs, and Sir Jeffrey stopped briefly to catch his breath. In the moment of silence that followed, Lucy heard a strange sound—the creaking of a floorboard and the slight rattle of a doorknob just inside a nearby room. Puzzled, she turned her head to look. Then her uncle started speaking again.

"He seemed anxious to arrive as soon as possible, although I'm a little confused as to why he's decided to come now. He's never wanted to visit before and I understand that when he contacted the foundation last year to offer us all that money, he was quite adamant about remaining anonymous. I wonder why he's chosen this exact moment to reveal his identity?" Sir Jeffrey suddenly looked concerned. "You don't think he's coming to see how we're spending his funds, do you Lucy? Oh goodness!" he continued, sounding flustered. "I didn't think of that before! All that money! It's such a responsibility! We do have a full accounting of everything, don't we, my dear? All the receipts for travel and food; the men's wages and the equipment ..."

"Of course, Uncle Jeff," Lucy interrupted, sighing. "I've personally recorded every item. The money's all accounted for, down to the last penny. The books are balanced, as usual."

"Thank goodness for that," Sir Jeffrey replied. He smiled sheepishly at her as he resumed his slow progress toward their rooms. "I'm sorry, Lucy. How could I have ever doubted it? You *are* a wonder!"

Lucy smiled back at him and shrugged, though her eyes soon wandered back to the door down the hall. Was it Darby's room, she wondered?

"I suppose it's actually quite fortunate that he's revealed himself now, isn't it?" Sir Jeffrey continued, his eyes sparkling even brighter. "We just might have something very remarkable to show him, if Mr. Darby's creature measures up!"

"Could Mr. Carew have heard about the capture somehow?" Lucy asked. "Is that why he's coming?"

"Well, I really don't see how," Sir Jeffrey replied. "We've just barely heard of it ourselves! And he's all the way back in Boston." Sir Jeffrey's expression slowly glazed over, as if he were slipping deeper into a difficult puzzle. "It's a curious thing," he continued, knitting his eyebrows together, "that he knew exactly where to track us down. Nepal is a big place. How on earth could he have known that we were staying here, in Dhunche, and at this particular hotel? And on the telephone just now, he enquired about my health—even though I've gone to great lengths to keep my current medical condition private. I haven't even informed the foundation! It's out of fear, I'm embarrassed to admit! I'm terrified that they'll decide I'm too old to manage these gruelling expeditions." Sir Jeffrey smiled sadly as he tapped the top of his bandaged foot with the end of his walking stick. "It's a bit of a mystery, isn't it? I'm quite positive that the only other person here who knows about my medications is Mr. Darby ..."

This time, a strange muffled thud came from behind the door of the room down the hall. Lucy stopped and tried to listen, but Sir Jeffrey's continuous talking drowned everything else out. "We'll set things up in my room. We've let things slip while we've been sitting around here twiddling our thumbs, haven't we? We've got to make this place look like a proper research station!"

Lucy opened her mouth to answer, but then stopped with a smile. Her uncle was speaking more to himself than to her. The door to his room was open now, and still the sound of his voice trailed out into the hall.

Lucy glanced back, one more time, before she turned to follow her uncle. All at once, the door down the hall swung open. Darby, looking furious, stormed out of the room and onto the landing. He stood frozen for a moment, still gripping the doorknob with his hand, red-knuckled and covered in flecks of dust. Lucy could just see past him and into the room where a big piece of yellow plaster was laying crumbled on the wooden floor, right below a fist-sized hole in the wall. Darby quickly pulled the door shut behind him.

"That was a lovely bath," he crooned, staring directly at Lucy. "Especially after waiting such a long time for it."

Lucy swallowed hard. "It must have been the shortest bath in history, Mr. Darby," she remarked.

"Ah, yes. Short but sweet, Miss Parnell," he replied, flashing a smile. "Just like you." He immediately turned and headed down the stairs.

Flustered, Lucy hurried into her uncle's room and closed the door firmly behind her. She stepped back and leaned all of her weight against it.

"I think we'll put the big spot lamp over there," Sir Jeffrey said, pointing to one corner. "What do you think?"

"Yes, fine," Lucy replied absently.

The encounter with Darby had left her feeling more than a little uneasy. She paced about the room while her uncle continued discussing his plans, finally wandering over to the window to peer through the thin cotton drapes. It was still quite early in the morning, with hardly anyone up and moving yet, which made the sight of a big, scruffy man leaning against the stone doorway on the opposite side of the narrow street all the more startling. He had a huge gash across his chin and a black eye the size of a grapefruit. Lucy pulled back from the windowsill for a second before cautiously peering out again. She'd seen the man somewhere before, of that she was certain. It was one of Darby's men, she remembered—Tyrone. But what had happened to him? Had he been in an accident? Why wasn't he with the other men? And why he was glaring up at Francis Darby's hotel window with a look of such sinister resolve? Tyrone was cradling his right side with one arm, casually puffing on the stump of a cigarette. He blew tiny circles of smoke into the air, awkwardly balancing the end of the filter tip between one finger and a huge bandaged thumb. He seemed to wince in pain each time he shifted his body, and as he continued to stare up at the hotel, there was a look in his eyes that was so devilishly cold—so murderous—it took Lucy's breath away.

4

THE DIARY

EVAN McKAY RUBBED the steam off the bus window
with his elbow. He had been hoping to spot some exotic
wildlife along the way or an interesting land feature, at least,
but for the last three hours there had been nothing to look at
but mile after mile of fog and drizzle. He turned away from
the window, pressed his cheek against the rolled up rain
jacket he had fashioned into a pillow and sighed with bore-
dom. He would have happily dozed the last few hours away,
but the constant swaying of the bus and the frequent jarring
bumps as the vehicle's wheels made contact with every over-
sized rock and pothole that littered the way made it next to
impossible. And those disturbances were nothing compared
to the intermittent screams and gasps of the other passengers
each time the bus driver swerved too close to the edge of the
road. It was probably a good thing that the mist was obscur-
ing their view, Evan thought; had they been able to see the
steepness of their ascent more clearly they would have
screamed even louder.

"Want some music?" the man sitting in the next seat

dangled an iPod in front of Evan's nose.

"No thanks, Dad."

"Want to help me with my crossword, then?"

"You're kidding, right?"

"Game of cards?" Evan's father felt around in the inside pockets of his jacket. "I know I've got a pack on me somewhere."

Evan closed his eyes and shook his head. He could hear his father groaning with frustration.

"Ahhh, come on, Evan! Snap out of it, eh! What sixteen-year-old kid wouldn't jump at the chance of running off to a place like this at a moment's notice? If my dad had ever taken me to Nepal on a business trip when I was your age ..."

Evan opened his eyes and stared straight ahead. "Business trip? Grandpa was a lobsterman, Dad."

"Yes, I know that, Evan. But that's not really the point now, is it?"

"Well, it would just be weird, wouldn't it? I mean, what kind of business could a lobsterman have in a place like—"

"Just forget it!" his father snapped. "Okay?"

Good, thought Evan. The plan had worked. Maybe his father would stop bugging him for a while.

Evan closed his eyes again and pressed his face deeper into the jacket. Just two months earlier, life had seemed pretty normal. He had successfully navigated his way through another year of high school and had already started looking forward to spending the summer holidays with his friends in Montreal. Then his parents had dropped the bombshell of the century: they were separating. Ever since, life had been anything but normal. Evan's father, Alec, a freelance wildlife photographer, had signed on for a six-month stint with the World Wildlife Society in London, England. Evan's mother, Kathleen, had relocated to her parent's secluded Laurentian mountain cabin, an hour's drive north of the city. Evan found himself caught between two distant and very different worlds, with not much interest in being in either one. After many heated discussions, it was finally decided that he would spend the first half of his holidays in London with his father and the second half with his mother in Quebec, leaving a grand total of three days right before the start of school to spend with his friends. Evan was furious. His parents mess up their marriage and his summer gets destroyed. How was that fair? The "exciting" and "exotic" adventure he now found himself on had not even begun to appease him.

"You're certainly not the most exciting travelling companion, are you?" Evan's father grunted as he sorted through the brown leather camera bag at his feet. He pulled out a small book and tossed it into his son's lap. "Here. Why don't you make yourself useful, at least. Take a look at this and see if you can figure out the currency exchange. I'm no good at that stuff, you know. I'll end up tipping some guy a whole week's salary to carry our bags into the hotel, or something."

Evan shrugged and picked up the book—an old travel guide. The grubby little thing was worn out, almost to the point of total collapse. At least half of the inside pages had pulled away from the binding and a large portion of the back cover had been torn off. Someone had tried to patch the thing together, Evan could see, and on more than one occasion, by the looks of it. Several different types of see-through sticky tape had been applied to the loose pages and some pieces were so brittle and yellowed, Evan couldn't begin to imagine how old they must have been. To finish it off, a large piece of grey duct tape had been carefully moulded around the book's spine in an attempt to hold the whole mess together. Evan didn't know how his father expected him to work out the currency exchange. The entire world economy must have changed twenty times over since the book was published.

"Where did you get this thing, Dad? It's really ancient!"

"What? It's no good?"

"Well, maybe if you were planning to time travel to Nepal," Evan replied sarcastically. "Backward in time, that is."

"Hey ... sorry! It was the best I could do on such short notice. I got it off Roger Trenton, one of the guys at the office, when I ran down there to pick up the airline tickets. Apparently, his older brother spent a lot of time in Nepal a few years back. He went on a backpacking trip after graduating from college and got hooked on the place. He even ended up staying a year or two in some kind of monastery up in the mountains. He lived just like a monk, Roger said—no possessions or anything; nothing but the clothes on his back, and that book, I guess."

Evan moved the tips of his fingers over the book's pages as if they had suddenly become contaminated in some way. "It looks as if the guy must have slept with this thing under his pillow every night." Evan grimaced. "Or maybe it was his pillow."

"According to Roger, his brother took the whole monk thing pretty seriously," Evan's father continued. "Their parents begged him to come home and he did, for a while. But even after he returned to the West and started working he just couldn't get the place out of his mind. He journeyed back to Nepal after about a year and never went home again.

He left the book behind with Roger. The family would hear from him every now and then, but even that stopped after a while. Roger's not sure where he is now, or even if he's dead or alive. Come on, Evan, do us both a favour and look through the book. Maybe you'll find something interesting in there." Alec McKay paused, looking down at his watch. "Besides, we've got four more hours to go before we reach Dhunche—lots of time to read."

Evan rolled his eyes. "Really great news, Dad."

With each new agonizing bump in the road, Evan wished that they had stayed in Kathmandu instead. That had been the original plan, and when the plane began its descent through the clouds on their arrival at Tribhuvan International Airport, Evan had been pleasantly surprised. The teeming metropolis of Kathmandu lay at the juncture of two rivers, the Bagmati and the Vishnumati, both sacred to followers of the Hindu faith. For a place nestled in the shadow of the wild and foreboding Himalayas, it still appeared to have everything to offer the modern traveller: beautiful monuments, parks, temples and shrines, luxury hotels and restaurants, and exotic market squares, all in a fascinating melding of the old and the new. Evan got a much closer look at things when the taxi driver, who'd picked them up at the airport, began navigating his way through the city. There were many intriguing architectural arrangements here—old, crumbling structures side by side with contemporary buildings—situated along streets overrun with every possible type of transport: trucks, buses, cars, motor scooters, bicycles and rickshaws.

In the downtown cores of Western cities, it was rare to see animals running about, except for dogs and the occasional squirrel. Kathmandu, however, seemed to offer an extensive menagerie of creatures: monkeys, goats, water buffaloes and sacred cows, all sharing space with a colourful throng of people, constantly on the move. Sitting in the back seat of the taxi, Evan rolled the window down for a second, letting in a blast of warm air, heavy with a pungent odour. Evan sniffed cautiously, breathing in an odd mix of flower scent, incense, curry, cinnamon, ginger and car exhaust. He quickly rolled the window back up again. He was ridiculously hot, and by the time the driver had dropped them at the entrance to the Everest Hotel, Evan was starting to wonder whether anyone here had ever heard of air conditioning. But the sumptuous appearance of the hotel lobby began to dispel his fears, right up until the moment the desk clerk handed his father a note: "Change of plan," it had stated. "Unable to have you met in Kathmandu as arranged. Please proceed immediately to Dhunche by bus."

Feeling more like a prisoner now than a tourist, Evan steeled himself for the next inevitable pothole and reluctantly opened the book's front cover. On the first page, a standard colour photograph of Mount Everest rested just below the title: *Backpacking through Paradise: Trekking Nepal in the Age of Aquarius*. An odd title for a travel guide, Evan thought. His eye wandered to a line that had been scrawled in pen just above it: Jack Trenton, August 1967. Next to that was a circular symbol with a line down the middle and two shorter ones branching out diagonally from the centre point. Evan thought he recognized it from somewhere. It looked sort of like the hood ornament from a Mercedes Benz. He nudged his father in the side and shoved the book under his nose, pointing to the odd symbol.

"It's a Ban the Bomb sign," said his father, glancing up from his crossword. Then his eyes fell on the signature. "Hey, it's dated August 1967. I didn't realize Roger's brother was here in the summer of love!"

"The what?"

"Don't tell me you've never heard of the summer of love!"

Evan shrugged.

"You know—peace marches, hippies, flower power and all that stuff?"

"I'm not sure. Maybe."

"Well, it was only one of the greatest times in the socio-political history of modern Western culture, Evan," his father continued with exasperation. "Good grief! What are they teaching you in school these days, anyway? You know, I remember when ..."

Suspecting that his father was about to embark on a long dissertation about his involvement in the summer of love, Evan quickly pulled the book away and pretended to start reading. Out of the corner of his eye, he could see that he was being watched. But with no audience to captivate, Alec McKay soon abandoned whatever it was he was going to say and returned to his crossword.

Figuring that four hours would pass a lot faster if he did something besides stare out the window at the fog, Evan decided that he might as well give in and do a little reading after all. At the table of contents, he skimmed over the usual travel guide headings: history, geography, climate, social structure, religion, politics, flora and fauna. Flipping through the introductory pages, he stopped every now and then when something interesting caught his eye. The national bird of

Nepal was the danphe pheasant, he discovered, though it could just as well have been the pigeon or the sparrow, judging by the thousands upon thousands he had seen infiltrating every city square, every monument and every underpass in Kathmandu. The national flower was the rhododendron—a rather uninteresting choice, Evan thought. He would have expected a much more exotic selection here, considering he'd just come from England, a place where you couldn't turn a single street corner without colliding with at least one giant rhododendron bush. Next, Evan discovered that the word *namaste*—spoken with head bowed and hands clasped in prayer—meant "welcome." That, he concluded, was a phrase that might come in handy later.

The following section of the book took a more intimate look at certain aspects of the country, dividing it into its many distinctive regions and zeroing in on the best places to do what most people generally go to Nepal for—trekking and climbing. In just the first few pages, Evan discovered that even though the Nepalese people themselves were seasoned trekkers, having utilized a vast system of walking trails for generations as trade and seasonal migration routes, the whole business of tourist trekking was only in its infancy in the late 1960s. In Jack Trenton's time, backpacking your way through Nepal would have been considered new and daring and a little crazy, the perfect indulgence for a hippie kid on a spiritual quest. Skimming through the sections devoted to the pleasures and perils of trekking, Evan wasn't convinced that he would have liked it at all. The rewards of exploring such a spectacularly beautiful and culturally rich area were undeniable. But the warnings about avalanches, the unpleasant side effects of drinking unpurified water, the monsoon season with its mudslides and leeches, and the complications brought on by altitude sickness made him cringe. Evan shuddered a little as he did a quick mental review of what one might expect to encounter on a trek out here: sudden mountain storms, contaminated water, rabid dogs and monkeys, altitude-induced hallucinations, liquid on the brain, air bubbles in the lungs, blood-sucking leeches the size of rats—actual rats —and, of course, the ever-impending threat of some sort of severe intestinal disorder. It made the North American canoeing adventures he'd been on seem like strolls through the park.

"You're not planning on doing any of this trekking stuff while we're here, are you Dad?" Evan suddenly blurted out.

"Well, I wasn't expecting to," his father replied. "It was going to be straight in, find this Sir Jeffrey Parnell person, take some shots of whatever he's found, and back out again—unless of course you'd like to stay on a bit longer. We could call one of those trekking outfitters and see what kind of packages they have this time of year, if you want. We did the Society a big favour coming here on such short notice. I'm sure they wouldn't mind footing the bill for a few extra days and—"

"No, Dad," Evan interrupted with a grimace. "Really ... it's okay."

Evan's father appeared a little disappointed. "Well, whatever you want. Oh, and by the way," he continued, "Roger Trenton wants that book back. It's all he's got left of his brother, so be careful with it, eh? I promised him we'd look after it like it was gold. Apparently, there are some notes written in the margins toward the back. He said Jack used that part like a personal diary. It might be interesting to read, actually, although Roger did warn me that it gets a little nutty at times. He said his brother always claimed to be a bit psychic. But Roger figured it was the effects of the high altitude or maybe even some crazy stuff that Jack was into smoking back then."

Evan turned to his father and raised his eyebrows.

"Hey, it was the sixties, right?" his father replied, shrugging.

Evan rolled his eyes at the comment, but he was intrigued by this new information. Leafing through the second half of the book, he discovered lots of dated notations from 1967 and '68, including daily weather reports, observations on birds and animals, and some sketches of woolly yaks and smiling villagers, all with the ever-present Himalayas looming in the background. There was even a blurry rendition of the Abominable Snowman—front and side views—looking a bit like a bad police sketch. Had the guy actually seen one of those things, he wondered? Evan scanned the accompanying notes looking for an answer.

October 19, 1967: Didn't get much sleep last night. Heard more weird screaming around one or two o'clock. Strong garlicky smell, too. Sherpa guides are getting real nervous sniffing the air now. They say it's a "metohkangmi," for sure—their word for a giant snow creature, I guess. Went looking for signs at daylight, but early snows had covered everything. Had just started back to camp when something darted out from behind a rock face about two hundred and fifty feet in front of me. Thing must have been over seven feet tall, judging by the distance. Wished I had my camera on me, but got a fair look at it anyway. Still not sure if my eyes were playing tricks on me or not. Sketched what I could remember. Would have loved to have gotten closer. Will just have to wait and see what tonight brings. I've been having those creepy psychic feelings of mine again, too, just like I did when I was a kid. Something really wild is about to happen, I just know it.

This was very cool, Evan thought to himself. Maybe his father had been right after all; maybe there really was something redeemable about the little book. Evan had always been interested in tales of the bizarre and unexplained and this looked like pretty good *Ripley's Believe It or Not* kind of stuff. If Jack Trenton actually saw what he thought he saw, then maybe some things were worth the risks of a high-altitude trek. The next entry turned out to be even more fascinating.

October 20, 1967: *Night started with another crazy serenade. Ear-piercing screeches and wailing sounds loud enough to wake the dead! Sherpas are getting more jittery by the hour. One of them's already run off, and I don't know how much longer I can talk the rest into sticking around. Can't shake that thing I saw out of my mind, either. My whole head's aching with it. Don't think I'm going to feel much better until I find out what it was. I've asked the Sherpas hundreds of questions, but they just keep looking at me funny like they think I've gone crazy. Maybe I have! But if I could just find some kind of evidence that the thing was real ...*

Evan squinted at the page. The next part was difficult to decipher. Trenton, either delusional from lack of sleep or altitude sickness, or pushed to the brink of madness by whatever he'd just witnessed, had simply scrawled the final few sentences across the bottom of the page. With his hair prickling at the base of his neck, Evan followed the broken lines of Trenton's shaking hand with the tip of his finger.

... must have fallen asleep for awhile. Woke up to that howling sound again. Tent flap was rustling like mad—from the wind, I figured. Felt kind of groggy, so I turned over in my sleeping bag and tried to doze off, but I couldn't. That awful smell was in the air again—real strong this time. Heard something like heavy breathing just outside the tent, then felt a flicker of hot air against the back of my neck! My heart was pounding so loud I thought my eardrums were going to explode! Something big was leaning into the back of me! I looked down at the bottom edge of the tent. There was something poking under from outside: a huge toe, as big as a German shepherd's paw, covered in long, silvery grey hair! I tried yelling something—to call the Sherpas—but the words just wouldn't come out of my mouth!

Hardly believing what he was reading, Evan found himself transfixed by Trenton's next revelation. Whatever it was that had possessed the man at that moment—whether it was madness or exhaustion, or some kind of misguided bravado—Trenton did something then that most people in their right minds would never have dreamed of doing. Slowly pulling his arm out of his sleeping bag, Trenton leaned forward and grabbed the end of the huge hairy toe! What he heard next was such a hideous mix of horrifying screams and screeches and bellows—some of them his own—that

Trenton confessed he could remember little else. By the time his terrified companions had arrived at his tent, the creature had already taken flight, leaving Trenton shaken and gasping for air. Refusing to stay any longer, the Sherpas broke camp and insisted on leaving at the first rays of dawn. It wasn't until several hours later, according to his notes, that Trenton found some unusual strands of silvery grey hair on the surface of his sleeping bag. Was this the proof he had been searching for? Evidence that would tell everyone that he wasn't losing his mind? Trenton wrapped the strands in a cloth bandana and placed them inside the back cover of the book. He would have them analyzed upon his return to Kathmandu.

Evan quickly flipped through to the very end of the small book, hoping to find the unusual stash. But there was nothing. In fact, as Evan quickly scoured the rest of the notes in the book, he found not a single other reference to the strands of hair. There was little more about the incident with the creature, either. It was puzzling to say the least, and a bit annoying, too.

Evan turned back and continued to read. The next entry came right after Jack Trenton's terrifying encounter in the tent, as he and his companions were slowly making their descent from the high country.

October 23, 1967: ... can't really explain how I'm feeling after everything that's happened. Still can't shake it out of my mind, even when I'm sleeping. That crazy thing comes to me in my dreams! I'm not even sure now if any of it happened—if I really heard and saw what I think I did. It couldn't have been true ... could it? But when I grabbed at it, when I touched it and felt its life force pulsing against my hand, it was like a rush of electricity. What a weird feeling of power, like I could do anything I wanted to, or have anything I ever dreamed of. At first it was amazing—intoxicating—but now I only wish I could forget it; that I'd never touched it! Because all I can think about is finding that damned thing again....

Evan continued reading, but with an added sense of sympathy now. It was clear that the overwhelming desire to find the creature was causing Jack Trenton's anguish and distress to increase by the hour. On one hand, he seemed scared of its wild and unpredictable nature. On the other, Trenton seemed determined to come into contact with its mysterious "life force" again. Trenton, Evan sensed, was basically a good guy—a man of conscience, his father would say. But the encounter with the creature had caused a bitter struggle within him. Rationally, he knew it was probably better to leave well enough alone, but somehow he just couldn't.

October 24, 1967: *... my thoughts exhaust me, terrify me. I no longer have the strength to sweep them from my mind. I feel so driven to find this thing again—to grab hold of the strange power that surged through me before, and yet I know in my heart that I should push these thoughts away forever. Why do I feel so confused? It is as if there are two of me now—tearing at each other, pulling me first one way and then another! I would give anything to find peace from this torture!*

The rest of Trenton's diary entries were much less interesting—

rambling philosophical essays on the meaning of life and the purpose behind his own existence. A day or two later, he felt compelled to leave his Sherpa companions behind and strike out on his own. He made his way to one of the remote Buddhist monasteries in the high hills and stayed for several months. From the tone of his final few entries, Evan could sense that Trenton experienced some sort of life-altering revelation. There was a newfound sense of purpose and tranquility to his words. The tormented daily ramblings were replaced by thoughts and observations on life and the search for universal harmony. The words were simple, yet profound. Jack Trenton, it seemed, had finally found peace.

Toward the very back of the book, Evan discovered something unusual: a lengthy poem—a ballad—written out, just like the diary entries, in Trenton's own hand. It must have had some special meaning, for he had written it very carefully, all eleven verses. He had started writing—upside down—at the left page's bottom margin. The words trailed up the side of the page, across the top and down the middle of the book, curling up again along the left margin of the right page. The writing flowed across the top of that page, then wound down the side, finishing, finally, at the bottom corner of the right page. The poem was entitled "The Green Eye of the Yellow God," and attributed to a J. Milton Hayes. It was dated 1911. Evan began to read:

There's a one-eyed yellow idol to the north of Khatmandu,
There's a little marble cross below the town;
There's a broken-hearted women tends the grave of Mad
      Carew,
And the Yellow God forever gazes down.

He was known as "Mad Carew" by the subs at Khatmandu,
He was hotter than they felt inclined to tell;
But for all his foolish pranks, he was worshipped in the
ranks,
And the Colonel's daughter smiled on him as well.

He had loved her all along, with the passion of the strong,
The fact that she loved him was plain to all.
She was nearly twenty-one and arrangements had begun
To celebrate her birthday with a ball.

He wrote to ask what present she would like from Mad
Carew;
They met the next day as he dismissed a squad;
And jestingly she told him that nothing else would do
But the green eye of the little Yellow God.

"So, have you managed to figure it all out, yet?" Alec suddenly interrupted.

Evan stopped reading with a jolt, but not before his eyes had fallen onto something Trenton had scrawled—a note to himself—across the bottom of the page, right at the end of the poem: *Remember this, Jack!*

Flustered, Evan closed the book and looked at his father. "Figured what out?"

"You *know*, the currency thing."

"Ummm ... haven't found it yet, but I think I'm on to something," he quickly mumbled. "That money exchange chapter's gotta be in here somewhere, right?"

5

THE DISCOVERY

SIR JEFFREY CAREFULLY laid the limp creature at the centre of the table.

"Bring me something warm and dry to wrap it up in, Lucy! The poor thing's barely breathing. We'll have to try to get some nourishment into it, too. I'll see if I can find an eye-dropper in the supplies."

He hobbled to the corner of his room, eased himself down onto his knees and began rummaging in one of the boxes under the window. Lucy made her way along the hallway to the bathroom, returning a few moments later with an armful of thin, stained towels.

"It's a clever little devil, this one," Darby snickered as he flicked the tip of his finger at the creature's tail. "It's just playing possum, if you ask me."

Sir Jeffrey, hobbling his way back to the table, grabbed Darby firmly around the wrist before he had the opportunity to inflict any further torment.

"It's hardly *playing*, Mr. Darby!" he blurted angrily. "This animal is near death. The poor thing's seriously dehydrated,

I suspect, and with all the cold water drenching it's had to endure, quite possibly hypothermic, too!"

Appearing surprised at Sir Jeffrey's outburst, Darby stepped back from the table.

"Now, don't be getting yourself all riled up," he protested. "It was a long trek back and we're all tired. That thing attacked one of the men, you know. Gave him some nasty gashes. Just look at those claws—they're as sharp as needles. I figured if we didn't feed it for a while, it might calm down a bit and behave itself."

"Did you think to feed it at *all*, Mr. Darby?" Sir Jeffrey glared at his field assistant as he took one of the towels from Lucy's hands and gently wrapped the creature in it. "Or prevent it from nearly drowning in that wretched cage?" Sir Jeffrey could barely contain his anger now. "I'm aware that this can be a place of limited resources, Mr. Darby, but considering all of the funds at your disposal, I'm surprised you couldn't have procured some updated equipment, or a wildlife carrier that was watertight, at the very least!"

Darby, raising an eyebrow, didn't respond.

"And those needle-like claws, as you call them," Sir Jeffrey continued, "appear to be far better suited for plucking leaves out of trees than for scratching! And trees, I might add, that can't be found at the altitude at which you claim to have taken this creature. In fact, I'm quite sure that this particular animal is poorly equipped to survive in any territory higher than the foothills. I would have thought that a zoology student of your calibre and experience would know that. How it got all the way up to the high country is a mystery to me. And while we're at it, Mr. Darby, where is this injured employee of yours, anyway? I'd be most interested in taking a look at the man's wounds."

Darby paused before answering and Lucy was almost sure she could detect a faint smile at the edge of his mouth. "Well, that might be a bit difficult," he replied. "I've terminated his contract, you see."

"Terminated!" Sir Jeffrey shot back. "On what grounds?"

Again, Darby didn't answer immediately. He stared straight into Sir Jeffrey's eyes and pursed his lips. "I rather not say, actually. It's of a personal nature."

"That explanation is totally unacceptable, Mr. Darby!" Sir Jeffrey replied firmly.

"Well, if you must know," Darby began slowly, "I dismissed him for insubordination. His behaviour was disrupting my authority over the other men."

"Is that so?" Sir Jeffrey glared at him again. "Well, as you can see, I have more pressing matters to attend to right now. But this business isn't over, Mr. Darby. Let me assure you of that!" He leaned one hand on his walking stick and began searching in his pockets. "Where *is* that blasted dropper?" he muttered under his breath. "It must be in one of the bags downstairs." He turned to his niece. "Keep an eye on things here, Lucy. I'll be right back."

Sir Jeffrey had barely made his way out of the room before Francis Darby had moved close enough to Lucy to make her feel very uneasy.

"Well, I do seem to have upset the applecart, haven't I?" Darby said, whispering the words into her ear. Lucy tried to move away, but Darby stuck to her side like glue. "The old boy's going to burst a blood vessel going on like that. Don't know what's gotten into him. He should learn to relax, if you ask me." He smiled and slipped an arm around her shoulder.

"A bit of advice we could all follow, wouldn't you say?"

Lucy bristled against his touch. "Mr. Darby!" she cried. "If you don't mind!"

"No, I don't mind *this* at all, darlin'," Darby whispered. He placed his other hand on her waist and pulled her around to face him. "Come on now. It wouldn't kill you to be a little nicer to me, would it?"

Lucy wriggled out of Darby's arms as quickly as she could. "Touch me like that again, and I'll have you fired on the spot!"

"Will you now?" he stepped backward and grinned. "I don't think you've got the nerve, darlin'. You're not about to go upsetting your uncle when he's feeling so poorly. You wouldn't want to jeopardize the whole expedition, would you?"

Lucy, breathing hard with anger, glared back at him. Darby grinned.

"And I don't know what you're getting all upset about, anyway. It's not like I haven't seen you stealing a look at me now and then—batting those big brown eyes. Think I haven't noticed?"

Lucy felt ill. How could he possibly have noticed that? It was months ago and she'd been nothing but cold and distant ever since. Suddenly, she felt trapped, just like the poor creature lying across the room, wrapped up in an old towel. "That was before," she blurted out.

"*Really*?" Darby asked, raising his eyebrows. "Before *what* exactly?"

"Be ... before I found out what you're really like," she replied awkwardly.

"And what would that be?" Darby persisted, a grin sliding across his face. "Come on, Lucy. You're going to have to tell me all about it. The suspense is practically killing me."

Lucy hesitated. Darby was smirking again—staring straight into her eyes as if he could read her mind. There was no escaping him. "Someone who could be very cruel," she replied, trembling, "if he thought it might be amusing—"

A rustling sound drew Lucy's attention away from Darby and back to the object on the table. The edges of the towel slowly quivered as the animal inside began to stir. She rushed forward, catching the whole bundle just before it rolled off the edge. As she held it in her arms, she was surprised at how light it felt. It was like cradling a bag of feathers. She lifted a folded piece of towel away and stared down. The creature, conscious now, was looking up, blinking a pair of limpid green eyes at her. Lucy, immediately entranced, began to smile.

"I'd be careful with it if I were you, girl," said Darby, lifting his hand in warning. "It's a vicious little thing."

"I don't know what you're talking about," Lucy replied sternly. "Perhaps you're confusing viciousness with mistrust. It actually seems quite docile to me."

"What? Stand aside!" he insisted. "I'll show you!"

Darby moved closer, grabbing the other side of the towel and pulling it open. As soon as the creature laid its green eyes on him, it let out an impassioned squeak, dug its tiny fingertips into the fabric and struggled to free itself. Lucy quickly drew the towel around it again and stepped back.

"There! See?" Darby announced triumphantly. "I told you it was vicious!"

"Frightened is more like it!" Lucy snapped back. "And it appears to be something specifically about you that's upsetting it, Mr. Darby. Perhaps you should leave now."

"Oh, so *you're* the animal expert now, are you?" Darby rolled his eyes. "Fine, then. Have it your way." He turned and walked toward the door. "Just consider yourself warned. I was only trying to do my job, you know. I should have thought twice and left that wretched thing in the for—" Francis Darby suddenly stopped speaking. Lucy could see the muscles twitching at the side of his face.

"The forest?" Lucy asked, raising her voice. "So it was as my uncle suspected, then! And just exactly *where*, Mr. Darby, would that forest be? You *do* know that there are restrictions in place about taking animals from certain areas—"

"I'm quite aware of that," Darby interrupted sharply. "And I don't need a lecture from you, Miss Parnell, about local law enforcement. *That* was merely a slip of the tongue," he continued. "Nothing more. We found the thing way up in the high country, just like I told your uncle. I don't know how the devil it got up there, but ask any of the men, if you want. They'll tell you."

"Really? Well, I hardly think that men who fear you would be willing to risk—"

"Fear me?" Darby chuckled and raised his eyebrows. "Now why would you be thinking a thing like that?"

"I've seen how they look at you."

Darby laughed. "My, my, you do have a wild imagination, don't you? Understanding your place and who's in charge is hardly the same thing as fearing someone, is it?"

"I don't know, Mr. Darby. You tell me." Lucy took a deep breath. She stared him hard in the eyes. "You told my uncle that one of the men was attacked by the creature."

"That's right," Darby replied, shrugging.

"Was it Mr. Tyrone?"

"What if it was?"

"Well, I've seen him," Lucy hesitated, swallowing hard.

"Impossible!" Darby snapped. "I dismissed him yesterday! He should be halfway out of Nepal by now."

"I saw him in town—just this morning," Lucy replied. "And he seemed to have more injuries than a small animal like this could inflict."

The muscles in Darby's face started to twitch even more violently.

"I wouldn't know about that."

"No?" Lucy replied. "Well, I think my uncle might be very interested all the same. In fact, I think I'm going to go and tell him about it right now—all of it. About Mr. Tyrone, about where you *really* found the creature, and possibly about the reason it's barely clinging to life ..."

"Oh, I wouldn't be too quick to do that, my girl." Darby's voice had suddenly taken on a very ominous tone. It stopped Lucy in her tracks, on the way to the door, and gave Darby the opportunity to step forward and grab her firmly by the arm.

Lucy tried to pull away. "What do you think you're doing?" she cried. "I've warned you before, Mr. Darby! Put your hands on me again and I'll have you fired!"

"No you won't, Lucy," Darby whispered into her ear as he tightened his grip. "And do you want to know *why* you won't? It's because you care too much about Sir Jeffrey Parnell and his great reputation. It may look to the rest of the world like he's directing this little venture into the wilds, but he's not paying for the whole show, now, is he? You wouldn't want to be throwing a spanner in the works just before the big cheese arrives, would you? What would *he* say—A Mr. Carew, is it?"

"You know about *him*?" Of course, he did, thought Lucy. The strange noises in the hall as she and her uncle had been speaking, coming from the room that turned out to be Darby's. It all made perfect sense.

"I accidentally overheard you and your uncle talking before."

"*Accidentally*?"

"Well, of course," he replied, smiling. "You two should really learn to keep your voices down."

"That's it!" said Lucy, so angry now she could barely form the words. "I'm going to get my uncle right now and—"

"And *what*?" Darby interrupted brusquely, digging the ends of his fingers into her arm. "You obviously haven't been listening to me, have you, Lucy? I wouldn't want things to get unpleasant."

"What do you mean?"

"Well, let's just say that this little corner of the world can be a pretty perilous place if you don't pay enough attention. There are all kinds of dangerous predicaments a person could encounter: finding themselves in the path of a sudden avalanche, for example, or a suffocating mudslide, or perhaps even headed for a nasty tumble off a cliff—"

"Are you *threatening* me, Mr. Darby?"

Francis Darby smiled. "Heaven's no, Miss Parnell. What gave you that idea? I'm just fulfilling one of my many job requirements. Looking out for my employer's best interests, you might say. It would be a shame for someone as important as your uncle to have an unfortunate accident, especially in a place as remote as this. It might take hours, even days, to get adequate medical attention. It hardly bears thinking about, does it?"

Lucy couldn't believe what she was hearing. Suddenly the room began to spin. She felt ill—hot and flustered. She clutched the bundled towel closer to her chest, then reached out for the edge of a table to steady herself.

"You know, back in Belfast," Darby breathed deep into her ear, pulling her even closer, "I was quite a draw on the local boxing circuit. They used to hold a ladies' night every time I fought. All the lovely young things like yourself would come out just to see me in the ring. I had a pretty good future ahead of me, too, until I had a few run-ins with the law and my old mum packed me off to America to live with my Uncle Patrick. Didn't take me long to give *him* the slip though—"

"I don't recall seeing any of that information on your job application," Lucy responded, trying to regain her composure.

"No, I don't suppose that you would, Miss Parnell," he replied, his voice as smooth as silk. "It will just have to be another one of our little secrets, won't it? Isn't it nice how we seem to be growing so much closer?"

The animal began to stir again just as Lucy heard her uncle struggling up the stairs. Darby heard him, too. Releasing his grip on Lucy's arm, he raised his eyebrows at her again. "Now, you won't be going and forgetting about our little conversation, will you, darlin'? We wouldn't want anything nasty happening to anybody."

"Found it!" Triumphantly holding a slightly bent eyedropper in one hand, Sir Jeffrey entered the room. He glanced at the towel Lucy was clutching so tightly. "What's happened? Is it?—"

"It's all right, Uncle Jeff," Lucy replied, watching Darby out of the corner of her eye. Her mouth was so dry, she could barely get the words out. "It seems to be awake now, actually."

As if in response, the animal wriggled in her arms.

"Excellent! Considering its initial condition, I wasn't expecting it to come around quite so soon. You must be having a positive influence on it, Lucy. We should probably give it something to eat now and then extract some quick blood samples, before it becomes too active."

When Sir Jeffrey peeled the towel away from the animal's body, its eyes, somewhat brighter now, frantically searched the room. Focussing on Darby's face again, it let out another loud and frantic squeal.

Startled, Sir Jeffrey stepped backward. "Goodness!" He turned and stared hard at Francis Darby. "Well, Mr. Darby, it seems to have taken quite a dislike to you!"

"No accounting for taste," Darby said flatly, as he headed for the door. "I'm leaving now, anyway. I still have some business with the men to attend to." As he passed by Lucy, he deliberately brushed up against her.

"Don't forget our little talk," he hissed into her ear. "And mum's the word."

Lucy swallowed hard and stared straight ahead.

Darby closed the door behind him. The old wooden floorboards creaked as he made his way along the hall and down the stairs.

"What was Mr. Darby saying to you just now?" Sir Jeffrey inquired.

"It was nothing," Lucy responded quietly.

"Well, I must say that I'm beginning to have some doubts about that young man," he replied. "His behaviour of late has been most unprofessional—the dreadful condition of the animal, then dismissing one of the men without even consulting me. Surely we can find another suitable field assistant somewhere. You'd think there would be dozens of graduate students beating down the doors for such an opportunity. I did think it was rather curious at the time that Mr. Darby was the only applicant ..."

"You shouldn't worry so much about things like that," Lucy interrupted. "Mr. Darby is probably just tired after the long journey back. I'm sure everything will work out fine."

Lucy spoke mechanically, keeping her eyes focused straight ahead. If she looked at her uncle now, she feared, she would lose her composure for sure. Sir Jeffrey's intention to dismiss his field assistant, news that just hours ago would have been music to her ears, was no longer an option. Dozens of distressing images plagued her thoughts, but none was as vivid as the sight of her beloved uncle's crumpled body lying at the bottom of a mud-filled, leech-infested gorge somewhere in the Himalayan foothills.

Lucy shuddered. In a strange twist, she had just become Francis Darby's unwilling defender—at least until she could figure a way out of the situation. Suddenly, she remembered Melville Carew. He would be arriving soon! Lucy felt a small glimmer of hope. Perhaps he could help! Surely, a man like Carew wouldn't tolerate Francis Darby's threats and self-serving attitude. After all, he was a man passionate enough about the cause of wildlife conservation to fund her uncle's expeditions and to come all the way to Nepal, wasn't he? That was it then. Lucy would simply take matters into her own hands—and their generous benefactor into her confidence—as soon as she could.

For the next few hours, Lucy assisted her uncle with his work, relieved to focus her attention on something other than Francis Darby. She carefully watched her uncle as he attended to the needs of his new patient. Lucy could see his excitement mount as he toiled to stabilize the animal's vital signs. It was unlike anything he had ever encountered before, he crowed repeatedly, enough to give an old scientist like himself, with decades of experience in the field, a substantial jolt.

Lucy, too, was captivated by the animal, and it soon appeared that these feelings were mutual. As long as she stayed within sight, it remained calm and compliant. As soon as she wandered away, however, it would stiffen up and deliver a barrage of forceful squeals until she returned. Although its odd appearance took a bit of getting used to, Lucy soon grew to find it rather amusing. It reminded her of the "Mr. Potato Head" toy she had once been given as a little girl, with its round, brown, potato body and dozens of inter-changeable plastic parts—ears, noses, feet and hands—that allowed her to create an unlimited number of bizarre combi-nations. It was a weird mixture of a number of animals, appearing to cross the boundaries of many different species—from the colourful feathers that sprouted out of the top of its head down to the lizard-like skin covering its hands and feet. It had a face and tail similar to that of a New World spider monkey, but its green, almond-shaped eyes were more akin to those of a wild cat. Mounds of soft fur covered most of its body, tipped with golden strands that shimmered in the light, but just below its pointed bat ears were two small slits, like the gills of a fish. It was as if someone had orchestrated an elaborate joke, Lucy's uncle suggested—like a zoological Dr. Frankenstein somewhere had decided to sew a few different animal parts together and give everyone a good scare.

Somewhat lulled by the gentle attention he was now receiving, the Creature assumed the worst of his ordeal had passed. He relaxed a little, turning his head back and forth to take in every detail of the strange place in which he suddenly found himself. He was feeling relieved and much calmer now; his stomach was full, the foul-smelling mud had been rinsed out of his fur and his body was once again warm and dry. The voice of the human creature nearest to him seemed pleasant and calming, too, like one of the morning birdsongs that echoed through the trees when the first rays of dawn light trickled down. It was not at all like the harsh and frightening sounds he had heard throughout the long hours of the night as he lay shivering, slipping in and out of dark sleep. This human's scent was not the pungent and unpleasant one he had encountered on the others either, but sweet and pleasing, like mountain wildflowers. Even so, the Creature's heart still hurt. Though his physical wants had been attended to for now, he ached to be with the Other. No one but she could ease the deep gnawing pain he still felt inside. He knew he would never be able to rest—never be truly at peace—until he was with her again. And with that troubling thought, he hung his head low and sighed, feeling a blackness of despair surround him. It would take nothing short of a miracle, he feared, for him to find his way back home now.

6

THE VISITORS

"MR. McKAY, I PRESUME? I'm Jeffrey Parnell."

Evan watched as his father smiled and extended his hand. "A pleasure, Sir Jeffrey. I'm Alec McKay," he replied. Then he quickly stepped aside. "This is my son, Evan. He's been spending some of his summer holidays with me in London. This Nepal trip was an unexpected bonus for us, wasn't it Evan?"

Sir Jeffrey shook Evan's hand and smiled warmly. "I must apologize for not greeting you in the lobby, gentlemen, but as I'm sure you've already noticed," he said, tapping his swollen, bandaged foot, "it takes considerable effort to navigate the stairs. I had no idea we would receiving two distinguished guests this evening! Fortunately, this time of year is not the busiest here, as the monsoons can be quite challenging. I'm sure the innkeeper will be able to accommodate an extra—"

Oh great, thought Evan. It was bad enough that his father had dragged him out into the middle of nowhere, but now they weren't even expecting him! Wonderful.

A look of embarrassment swept across Alec McKay's face. "I hope we haven't caused you any inconvenience, Sir Jeffrey," he interrupted. "I just assumed that the London office would have informed you that I was bringing my son along."

"Think nothing of it, Mr. McKay. It's quite alright," Sir Jeffrey replied. He gestured for them to enter his room. "Actually, I always find it a pleasure to have young people around." He turned to Evan. "My niece Lucinda must be about your age. You'll be able to meet her later. It may take a while until we're ready for you and your camera, so until then, I would suggest you both take the opportunity to get some rest. That road trip in from Kathmandu isn't the most comfortable, is it?"

"I'll say," Evan's father replied, settling into one of the room's two chairs, across from Sir Jeffrey. Evan wandered over to the window and pushed aside the faded curtain. The street below was practically deserted. "But the country's magnificent," his father continued. "The views must be spectacular when the weather's clearer, eh?"

Sir Jeffrey smiled warmly again. "I wasn't aware that you were a Canadian, Mr. McKay."

"Now, how did you figure that out, *eh*?" Evan's father grinned back.

"Just a lucky guess! Before we settle you in your rooms, though, I'd like to get down to some business. I'm not certain what the foundation told you when they offered the photography assignment, Mr. McKay, but it appears that we have a fascinating zoological find on our hands. We'd like you to document an animal that was discovered at one of the higher altitudes. Whether this turns out to be a new species, an anomaly of nature or an isolated mutation of some sort hasn't yet been determined. The poor thing was not brought to us in the best of conditions, I'm afraid to say, although we are attempting to rectify that situation now. My niece and I have decided to name it a 'carew,' for reasons I will divulge later. The scientific name is going to take a little longer to pinpoint, as the animal possesses a number of features that will make it difficult to accurately classify. I think you'll understand what I'm talking about when you see it for yourself."

"Did you say carew?" Evan asked, speaking for the first time. He'd been staring out the window as his father and Sir Jeffrey spoke, but the familiar word had grabbed his attention. "That's really weird. I was just reading something on the bus that had that name in it. This guy wrote out a poem in an old guidebook about someone called Mad Carew ..."

"Ah, yes," Sir Jeffrey remarked, "written almost a hundred years ago, during the Raj—the time of British rule in India. It's about the misfortunes of a soldier stationed there."

Evan nodded his head. He turned away from the window and took a seat on the only surface left available—the bed. "Yeah, that's it."

"I'm actually rather familiar with the piece, young man," Sir Jeffrey continued. "But, if you don't mind, I would appreciate it if you could refrain from mentioning it over the next few days."

Evan looked quizzically at his father and then back at his host.

"If you promise to keep it under your hats, gentlemen, I'll let you in on a little secret. You'll know about it soon enough, I suppose." Sir Jeffrey had lowered his voice to a whisper. "The money that's been funding many of our recent expeditions, including this one, has come from another Carew altogether—the famous Melville Carew, in fact. And I have just recently discovered that he is on his way here—now—to visit with us!"

"*Carew*? The billionaire?" Alec McKay all but shouted the words, and Evan stared at him blankly. What were they talking about?

"Multi-billionaire, actually," Sir Jeffrey replied. "He initially intended to remain an anonymous donor to our cause. I have only just learned his identity myself. Now that we have made what may turn out to be a significant discovery, it is only fitting, in my estimation, that we mark his great contribution to science by naming our new find after him. My niece concurs and has agreed to help me convince him. Mr. Carew has been quite determined to avoid the limelight so far, but I do hope that after all he has done for us, he will agree to accept our surprise gift."

"Who wouldn't!" Alec exclaimed. "That's quite an honour, eh? Having an animal named after you?" He turned to face his son. "I bet you didn't think you'd run into someone as famous as Melville Carew here, did you?"

"Who's Melville Carew?" Evan asked.

Alec rolled his eyes with embarrassment.

"You're not *serious* are you?"

Evan shrugged his shoulders.

"He's quite famous in certain circles," Sir Jeffrey interjected. "His career in the world of high finance has been well-documented over the past few decades. Quite by coincidence, I read an article about him the other day in a December issue of *The Wall Street Journal*. Fascinating! Melville Carew is listed as one of the ten richest people on the planet."

"Now, if you asked Evan to name the top ten rock guitarists in the world," Alec sighed, "he'd reel them off without blinking."

"Dad!" Evan protested.

"The young have their own idols, I suppose," Sir Jeffrey replied, smiling. He turned to Evan. "Any fascination with Melville Carew is no doubt limited to my generation or older. He is, after all, almost ninety-six."

"And he's travelling all the way to Nepal?" Alec exclaimed. "I can't imagine that the altitude here would be all that good for a man of his age. I'm half that and I'm having trouble catching my breath."

"I understand he's no normal ninety-six-year-old," Sir Jeffrey replied. "He paid for a twenty-million-dollar trip to the international space station when he was eighty-eight, then travelled in a submersible to view the wreck of the Titanic the following year. Add that to his annual 'around the world' yacht races, those gruelling trans-Sahara car rallies he fancies and back-to-back tours of the Arctic and Antarctic and you have, I suspect, anything but your average senior citizen."

"Wow," Evan mumbled.

"He appears to have led a most fascinating life," Sir Jeffrey continued, "and not surprisingly, he also has a keen interest in matters of health and aging. He's supposedly spent millions on every kind of potion and lotion and remedy available in an attempt to remain as young and vital as possible. He was one of the leading investors in cosmetic Botox, you know, and one of the first to use it, too. The article says he had a face like a Shar-Pei puppy just ten years ago, and today there's hardly a wrinkle at all. Now, there *have* also been some rumours that he's indulged in some other ...

um ... shall we say, unconventional medical practices, but he refuses to comment on them."

"Like what?" Evan asked, intrigued.

"Mummification, apparently," Sir Jeffrey replied. "Carew's rumoured to have funded research into the practice for a number of years now, hiring medical teams to replicate ancient Egyptian embalming techniques with current scientific modifications. That along with his obsession with Egyptian reincarnation beliefs and burial rituals—plus a few other macabre interests—has only served to fuel a great deal of speculation about the man. He's been called weird and eccentric on more than one occasion, as you might imagine. But that aside, I think we should be grateful that his interests have extended into our humble little world."

"What, you mean 'save the whale' kind of stuff?" asked Evan.

His father groaned. "I'm sure Sir Jeffrey was referring to environmental causes and wildlife preservation."

"It's not general knowledge," Sir Jeffrey replied, chuckling. "Though I am not about to question anything that aids our cause. Perhaps this is something he has always felt strongly about. Since he clearly has the money to support these expeditions, I am only too pleased accept it. It isn't easy to raise funds for these little outings into the wild. Perhaps there is something in Mr. Carew's past that has tweaked his interest—a passion to assist the underdog, perhaps?"

"Or find the extinct dog," Evan chimed in.

Sir Jeffrey laughed.

"What other ... um ... macabre interests does Mr. Carew have?"

"Cryonics, for one."

"Huh?" Evan muttered.

"Freezing," his father interjected. "He probably wants to have his body preserved after death. Some people have been doing that in the hope that they can be resuscitated sometime in the future, when there's a cure for what they died of."

Sir Jeffrey nodded. "Once again, though, Mr. Carew has taken a slightly different path. Apparently, he is intending to have just his *head* frozen."

"Gross!" Evan responded with a grimace. "Why would anyone do that?"

Sir Jeffrey shrugged. "He could be planning to plant it on top of a robotic body, I suppose," he replied, tapping his finger against his forehead. "Why bother to preserve a ninety-six-year-old body when most of what makes you 'you' is up here. Right?"

Evan tried to imagine this, and found that he couldn't. "But what good is a brain with no body—no arms, no legs, no heart? It's just a head then, not 'you,' right?"

"A very interesting question, young man," Sir Jeffrey replied, raising his eyebrows. "I suppose it would depend on how you feel about the soul and where it might reside." He suddenly chuckled. "Of course, this could all be supposition, too. Mr. Carew might only have been interested in thriftiness. I understand it costs sixty thousand dollars less just to freeze just one's head."

"Like someone *that* rich would care about saving sixty thousand dollars." Evan scoffed.

"Mr. Carew didn't get to where he is now by being reckless with his money," Sir Jeffrey replied. "He may be enormously rich, but I understand his beginnings were anything but impressive. He started life in poverty, but somehow ended up at Harvard University, rubbing shoulders with considerably richer and more privileged students. The father of one of my own classmates attended the school with him. Melville Carew, he once told us, had a reputation for straddling a very fine line between legitimate schemes and ones that bordered on the larcenous. Some of his money-making ventures were so insanely brilliant that he became the talk of the campus. He even acquired the nickname of 'Mad Carew'—a label he's never been able to completely shake off."

"Hey! Just like the poem, right?" Evan asked.

"Precisely," Sir Jeffrey replied.

"See! I told you this would turn out to be an exciting trip, Evan," Alec exclaimed. "Not only are you in Nepal, you're about to meet one of the wealthiest men in the world! You're going to get a private audience with old Mad Carew himself!"

"Please, Mr. McKay!" Sir Jeffrey cringed. "I understand that he absolutely *abhors* that reference! Apparently some of his fellow classmates had quite a bit of fun with that poem, changing some of the lines at poor old Melville's expense." Sir Jeffrey paused then and rubbed at his chin. "Now, how did the original go? It's been a while ... *He was known as Mad Carew by the* ... um ... ah ..."

"*Subs at Khatmandu,*" Evan continued for him. "*He was hotter than they felt inclined to tell. But for all his foolish pranks, he was worshipped in the ranks, and the Colonel's daughter smiled on him as well.*"

"That's it!" Sir Jeffrey remarked. "Well done, Evan!"

"I don't know what to say," Alec interjected, a look of surprise on his face. "I'm very impressed, son. I had no idea you had such an interest in poetry."

"Relax, Dad," Evan replied flatly. "It was an eight-hour bus ride, remember? I read that guide book over and over so many times, a lot of it's just stuck in my head now, I guess."

"That particular part, you see," Sir Jeffrey interrupted, "was altered into a little jab at Melville Carew, with the newer verse finding itself frequently performed as a party piece by friend and foe alike. I believe it went—*he was known as Mad Carew by the gang at Harvard 'U,' he was hotter than they felt inclined to tell; but for all his foolish pranks, he was worshipped by the banks, and the Fortune 500 smiled on him as well.*"

"Very creative," Alec commented.

"Lame," said Evan.

"The story goes that he initially took the ribbing and his new nickname with good humour," Sir Jeffrey continued. "It was just supposed to be fun, after all, and since he was well on his way to becoming one of the richest men on the planet at the time, one would imagine he didn't care that much. But apparently, something happened along the way. He grew to loathe that poem, flying into a rage anytime it was mentioned. That's why I felt the need to caution you about it, you see. If you could refrain from saying anything ..."

"I understand perfectly," Alec offered. "Don't worry about us." He turned to his son. "We'll keep our mouths shut, won't we, Evan?"

"Sure, Dad. Whatever."

All at once, the door swung open. A girl with dark hair, maybe his age, rushed into the room. This must be Sir Jeffrey's niece, thought Evan, trying to remember her name—Lisa ... Leslie ... Lucinda!

"Uncle Jeff! It's incredible! You won't believe what just—"

As the sleeve of Lucinda Parnell's stretchy cardigan

hooked itself onto a large piece of wood protruding from the doorframe, she was stopped short; then, as the piece of wood snapped off, catapulted backward out of the room. She landed on her bottom in the middle of the hallway. Picking herself up from the floor, she slowly crept forward on her knees and scanned the room. "I'm sorry, Uncle Jeff," she mumbled with embarrassment. Standing now, Alec McKay leaned over and gallantly offered her his arm. "I didn't know you had visitors."

"Our co-workers, actually," Sir Jeffrey replied. "This is Alec McKay, the wildlife photographer we've been expecting, and his son, Evan. Gentlemen, this is my niece, Lucinda," Sir Jeffrey looked down with concern. "You haven't injured yourself in any way, have you, my dear?"

The girl blushed, shook her head and smiled weakly. It was an awkward moment for her—for everyone there, in fact—but Evan, for reasons he could not fathom, felt compelled to let out a hearty laugh. Even as it was happening, he could feel the cold glare of his father's eyes bearing down on him and a strong elbow in his side, and he knew instantly that he was in serious trouble. His inappropriate behaviour might have been due to the long and exhausting bus trip, or perhaps it was the side effect of being somewhere new and strange. Whatever the reason, it was inexcusable. In deference to his niece's feelings, Sir Jeffrey pretended not to notice the outburst. The girl, however, turned to Evan and glared at him with a look so harsh and withering he wanted to sink into the floor.

Thankfully for Evan, everyone's attention quickly turned away from him and back to the reason for Lucy's spectacular entrance. Noting that the creature seemed more comfortable in his niece's presence than his own, Sir Jeffrey had transferred his new, comfortable enclosure into Lucy's room. Left in her care while Sir Jeffrey made arrangements to have some preliminary blood, fur and skin samples sent to a Kathmandu lab for biochemical and DNA testing, the creature appeared to have grown even more attached to Lucy. He had begun, she now reported with excitement, to emit a sound that could only be described as a deep purr.

"I know that cats do that when they're contented, although the exact anatomical source of the sound has been disputed for centuries, as you know," Lucy explained.

Evan raised one eyebrow.

"Of course, they can also purr when unduly stressed or in pain, correct?"

"That's right, my dear," Sir Jeffrey replied, nodding his head.

Lucy turned to Evan and his father. "Many researchers suspect that these low-frequency sounds and their accompanying vibrations may have some sort of comforting or even curative effect upon felines, although this has never been scientifically proven." She took a deep breath. "With the current data that's available to us, of course."

Alec smiled blankly at her. Evan raised his other eyebrow.

"I think we can all quite readily agree," Lucy continued, "that this animal is, almost conclusively, not a cat, per se, based on our understanding of that species' physiology. Although, it might be that it still has some ancient connection to *Smilodon*."

"Indeed," said Sir Jeffrey.

"Huh?" Evan grunted.

Lucy turned in Evan's direction. "Phylum Chordata, class Mammalia, order Carnivora, family Felidae, subfamily

Machairodontinae, genus *Smilodon*. Having lived during the Pleistocene Epoch and named by Plieninger in 1846."

Evan stared blankly.

"Prehistoric cat?" Lucy continued. "You know—the sabre-toothed tiger? You might better remember it as one of the Flintstone's house pets."

Evan was almost sure that he had just been insulted.

"Anyway," Lucy continued, turning away, "I had just finished making some notes in our journal, Uncle Jeff, when something truly amazing happened. I thought I would try offering the animal a few slices of tinned mango through the enclosure bars. As I was doing this, it suddenly closed its eyes and reached one of its hands toward me. The expression on its face was quite blissful—"

"Wow," Evan interrupted. "Animals have facial expressions, huh?" There was the shadow of a smile on his lips. "I didn't know about that stuff, either. But I suppose you're going to tell us that information's been documented in some scientific journal somewhere, right?"

Lucy glared at him before she continued. "When it lifted the fruit to its mouth, the purring became significantly louder, and when it started licking up the juice that was dripping down its arm, I could see its tongue for the first time—long and pink and forked, like a snake's!"

"So you've definitely determined that it's a cross between a cat *and* a reptile, then, right?" Evan asked.

"Well ... no ... I'm not saying that," Lucy stammered, glaring at Evan again. "I don't know what it is," she suddenly snapped. "It has many features."

Evan shrugged. "Hey, I was just asking." It might be better, he decided, to keep his mouth zipped for awhile. But at least he'd managed to rattle the girl. Good. It served her right.

Flustered now, Lucy tried to continue with her story. "Then, the most fascinating thing happened! At first, I thought I was imagining it, but the longer I looked, the more certain I became. You know those deep cuts on its hands? Well, they were slowly knitting together. And the bruises on its arms were starting to fade, too! It looked so peaceful just then. I reached my hand through the bars and touched the end of one of its fingers. It eyes suddenly flashed wide open. They were deep green and glowing—not like before. I've never seen anything like them. They were piercing and full of fire, like two bright, burning emeralds." Lucy paused then, to catch her breath.

She needed to decide whether to tell them what had happened next. It was so strange, so unexpected, that she didn't know what to think. But of course, her uncle needed to know. She glanced at the blond-haired boy—Evan?—sitting on the bed. She wished with all her heart that he wasn't there. She took a deep breath and continued. "I just sat there on the floor, staring into his eyes—they were so beautiful! And then, something flashed into my mind—images of another place. It was a place that I'm sure I've never been to before, and yet it seemed oddly familiar. There was mile upon mile of thick treetops, streams of cascading water and bright, warm sunlight. I started to feel sleepy, the way I imagine people being hypnotized might feel, but I wasn't afraid. It was as if I was receiving a message from somewhere—from the animal, I think. It was as if he was saying 'thank you.' Not in words exactly. I just seemed to sense what he wanted me to know."

Sir Jeffrey eyes were sparkling with anticipation. "And ...?"

"He's feeling much better now," Lucy continued. "But his heart is full of great sadness."

Rolling his eyes, Evan had to turn away. He couldn't believe what he was hearing! What was this—some kind of animal telepathy? She had to be kidding! On top of being clumsy and rude, the girl was crazy, too! The irresistible urge to laugh out loud suddenly returned. But he couldn't do that—not again! It would have been unforgivable. Besides, his father would flatten him. Evan quickly put his hand up to his mouth and prayed that something would intervene.

"Evan? Are you feeling okay?" his father asked. Sir Jeffrey and the girl were staring at him. "You look a little strange, son."

"Um ... uh ..." mumbled Evan from behind his hand. "Sick ..." he finally uttered.

"Last door on your left, end of the hall," Sir Jeffrey offered hastily.

Evan's father took his son firmly by the shoulders, hurried him to the doorway and turned him in the direction of the bathroom.

"Don't feel too bad, young man," Sir Jeffrey called out after him. "It sometimes takes a while for the digestive system to adjust!"

Racing down the hall, Evan was determined not to remove his hand from his mouth until he had safely locked the bathroom door behind him. With his back to it, he slowly let himself slide all the way down until he was sitting cross-legged on the old tiled floor. It was then that he began to laugh uncontrollably again. Here he was, after all, in the strangest place he could imagine—after enduring the bus ride from hell—forced to listen to some insufferable girl babble on about her bizarre "mind-melding" experiences with an odd little animal. It was completely insane! His friends back home would never believe it.

Evan stood up and stared into the small mirror above the sink, brushing aside the stray strands of curly blond hair that had fallen into his eyes. He turned on the tap. There was a loud groaning sound in the pipes before a little spurt of yellowish water, smelling strongly of sulphur, burst out of the faucet. Evan cupped some of it in his hand. He sniffed at it suspiciously for a few seconds before grimacing and releasing it down the drain. He reached across the sink and pulled a small, grubby-looking towel off a big thumbtack that was stuck into the wall. He examined it thoroughly, back to front, before cautiously wiping away the tears of laughter that had pooled in the corners of his eyes.

By the time Evan had composed himself enough to make his way back down the hall, everyone else had wandered through to Lucy's room to look at the recovering animal. It had fallen asleep, flat on its back. With lizard arms and legs outstretched with abandon, it was purring contentedly, like a kitten. It's fur-covered stomach bulged with the entire contents of a large tin of sliced mangoes in heavy syrup. Most of the plumes at the top of its head had dried out and were cascading now down its sides.

"Would you look at that, eh?" Evan's father commented.

"Remarkable little thing, isn't it, Mr. McKay?" Sir Jeffrey replied.

Evan nudged his way past his father, trying to get a closer look. A gentle breeze from the open window blew through the room, rippling across the creature's colourful head feathers. They looked, he thought, like the sweeping strands of summer wheat he'd seen in Saskatchewan last year, shimmering and dancing as they waved back and forth in the warm prairie wind. Evan hadn't expected to be impressed with the animal, but he realized suddenly that it was impossible for him to turn his eyes away. And he didn't feel much like laughing anymore, either. Not now. There was sadness in its heart, he remembered the girl saying. It was hard for him to believe such a thing, especially as he watched the creature's small furry chest rise and fall in a peaceful, rhythmic movement. In fact, nothing could have seemed further from the truth. But Evan knew all too well that things weren't always as they appeared. After all, he had been laughing himself to the point of tears just minutes before. But now, staring down at the animal, contemplating its capture and imprisonment and all the things about his own life that troubled him, he realized that there was suddenly a great heaviness in his heart, too. And when the time came for everyone to squeeze out of Lucy's room again and take a few moments to settle into their own, Evan hoped that no one had seen him trying to wipe away a tear of another kind that had pooled in the corner of his eye.

More exhausted than he'd ever felt before, Evan entered the room he had been allotted and slumped down onto the small, creaky bed. The room was extremely sparse by Western standards—a single, army-issue bed with a small, lumpy pillow and a thin, grey blanket. There was one old chair in a corner; its wooden legs chipped, its seat sagging from what must have been decades of use. Evan rolled over onto his side and stared blankly at the network of spidery cracks in the stained plaster wall.

His first encounter with the Parnells had been an altogether disastrous experience. He imagined that his father must be furious. While they'd been observing the animal in Lucy's room, Evan had tried to redeem himself. He'd even asked a few questions, trying desperately to promote any kind of intelligent conversation. But the girl would have none of it, probably convinced that he was nothing more than a rude and insensitive North American. After suffering her harsh stares and sarcastic comments for as long as he could, he'd finally given up, concluding that his mission of reconciliation was hopeless and that Lucinda Parnell was just one of those stuffy, humourless English girls.

Evan found himself tossing about on the edge of the narrow bed as he thought on all of these things. He heard a gentle knocking on the door next to his—Sir Jeffrey Parnell's room—and then his father's voice. Evan wasn't surprised. Alec McKay often had trouble sleeping, even more since the separation. On top of that, Evan could tell that his father was really pumped up about being in Nepal, about the photography assignment and, he imagined, the unexpected sight of such a bizarre animal. He heard Sir Jeffrey's voice inviting his father in and then suggesting tea. The walls in the old hotel must be unbelievably thin, Evan thought. He could hear almost every word. Too exhausted to listen any further, he finally closed his eyes and drifted off to sleep.

7

THE REVELATION

IN ANOTHER ROOM next to Sir Jeffrey's, on the opposite side to Evan's, Lucy sat on the edge of her own small bed, thinking about everything that had happened. She sighed and buried her face in her hands. As if her introduction to their new guests hadn't been humiliating enough, it appeared that she was now expected to endure the endlessly idiotic jokes and snide comments of a boorish boy from Canada. It was almost too much to bear. She glanced across the room to where the creature was still sleeping peacefully—alternately snoring and purring—in his spacious new enclosure in the corner. At least he had found some peace, however temporary.

Lucy couldn't even contemplate sleeping now. There was simply too much on her mind. In the end, she had told her uncle —and the McKays—almost everything about her strange encounter with the creature. But there was one part she felt compelled to keep to herself. In her heart Lucy knew that she had experienced something unusual—a communion so powerful and highly charged that there was almost an element of danger in having been witness to it. And it had left its mark on her. On top of being confused and overwhelmed, she now felt an irresistible urge to protect the animal, as if a great responsibility had suddenly befallen her. She didn't understand how or why, but she did know that she had been right to keep these impressions to herself. If she felt any guilt about misleading her uncle, it was tempered by the way he had looked at her while she explained the encounter. Had he been keeping something from her? He looked pale and worried, and she had no idea why.

Lucy laid back on her bed and stared at the ceiling. She heard a knock on her uncle's door, followed by the voice of the boorish boy's father.

"Have a seat, Mr. McKay," Lucy heard her uncle say. "I'll order us some *chiyaa* tea, if you'd like."

"Sure, that would be gr—" Alec suddenly stopping speaking.

Sir Jeffrey chuckled. "Don't worry. It's quite safe to ingest. We brought a large supply of bottled water with us from Kathmandu, and until that runs out, the hotel owner and his wife have strict instructions to serve us nothing else."

Lucy heard the door open again, followed by the sound of her uncle hobbling onto the landing. He shouted his refreshment order down the stairs.

"Quite a strange sight," Alec remarked, after his host had returned. "The animal, I mean. My other assignments have been on the more mundane side. This cryptozoology must be fascinating stuff, eh?"

"Both fascinating and frustrating, I'm afraid. These animals don't generally emerge from their habitats waving flags about so that we may easily find them. They are, for the most part, extremely secretive creatures. But there is always hope, I suppose. The world of cryptozoology will occasionally offer up a delightful surprise—a giant squid sighting, a different variation of dung beetle, perhaps a flesh-eating sponge or two. New creatures *do* seem pop up every now and then. Just a few years ago, two previously unknown species of monkey were found in the Brazilian Amazon. Then there's the case of the woolly flying squirrel. Once the largest squirrel in the world, it was long believed to be extinct, until it was recently rediscovered living in Northern Pakistan. The giant ivory-billed woodpecker in the southern United States is the most current addition to our 'returned from the dead' files; you may have read the news reports about it this past summer."

On her side of the wall, Lucy stifled a groan. Once her uncle got going, he could be hard to stop. She wondered if Mr. McKay knew what he'd gotten himself into.

"But sadly, Mr. McKay," he continued, "these discoveries are a drop in the bucket compared to the plants and animals that routinely appear on critically endangered lists or that disappear from the planet every day. But people prefer to hear about the living ones, I'm afraid, and the weirder and more bizarre, the better." Sir Jeffrey paused for a moment and sighed. "People always seem to want stories about carnivorous sea monsters or giant hairy apes or Mongolian death worms, don't they?"

"Mongolian death worms?" Alec exclaimed.

"Giant worms with deadly electrical powers," Sir Jeffrey replied, "or so the Mongolian desert dwellers who fear them will tell you. Five feet long and as red as blood, they only come out of their burrows for two months of the year—whenever it rains. But they can disable a camel in seconds with a spray of their toxic saliva before they finish them off with a powerful jolt of electricity."

"Seriously?"

"Those who claim to have encountered one of them—or have mysteriously lost a camel or two—will swear to it. See, Mr. McKay? It's very hard to resist a story like that, isn't it? Some unassuming little creature that's about to pass into oblivion isn't half as interesting. Nevertheless, the preservation of all living things is something in which every one of us should have a vested interest. It's imperative, you know. Our future—our very *lives*, in fact—may depend on it."

Lucy smiled. Despite the fact that she'd heard his speech countless times, she always loved to hear her uncle talk this way. If enough people with her uncle's passion and conviction put their minds to it, they might just be able to change the world one day.

Evan's father spoke again. "That photograph over there —the one that's propped up against the windowsill—may I ask who it is?"

Lucy swallowed hard. She could close her eyes and see every detail of that one picture—a formal, silver-framed portrait of a man and woman; she in an elegant evening gown, holding a cello and he, clad in a tuxedo, standing behind her. The woman's face, though older, was remarkably like her own.

"My younger brother and his wife," Sir Jeffrey replied. "Frederick and Rosalie were Lucy's parents. They were killed in a car crash when she was just three."

"I'm so sorry," Alec replied. "It must have been awful for you—and Lucy, too, of course." There was a pause in the conversation and then he spoke again, his voice softer now. "She was a musician?"

"Indeed. Rosalie was first cellist with the London Symphony."

"*Really*? She must have been very good to have played with an orchestra like that."

"My sister-in-law was a most exceptional young woman, Mr. McKay. Not only was she a talented musician, she was a gifted psychic."

A psychic? Not sure of what she had just heard, Lucy sat upright on the edge of the bed and held her breath. There was another knock on her uncle's door. Lucy groaned quietly and clenched her fists.

"Yes, thank you," she heard her uncle say. "Just put the tray down on the table over there, if you will."

The sudden and jarring sound of china shattering, followed by a muffled cry, floated through the wall. Lucy grimaced. The person who had delivered the tray of tea must have dropped something. She hoped it wasn't poor Maya again.

"Was that the fourth time this week, my dear?" her uncle asked. "Well, never mind. I'll take care of it."

Lucy could just barely hear his next words. "One more time," he practically whispered, "and I understand it's out on the street for the poor girl."

Sir Jeffrey hobbled onto the landing again.

"Tenzing!" he shouted down the stairs. "I'm dreadfully sorry, old man, but my blasted cane has had another unfortunate encounter with your crockery. Please send someone up with a broom and shovel immediately and add the cost of the damage to my account."

The soft tones of a young woman's voice filtered through the walls.

"Think nothing of it, my dear," Sir Jeffrey replied. "Heavens, it's only a saucer! Now, off you go."

The door to her uncle's room closed with a click. Lucy held her breath again, praying that the conversation would pick up where it had left off.

"I've never had *chiyaa* before," Alec remarked. "It's really quite good—hot and milky. Sweet like honey, too. Let's see ... I can taste ginger, I think, and cinnamon, too. But there's something else ..."

"Cloves and a dash of cardamom, I believe," Sir Jeffrey replied. "Delicious, isn't it? They do make a rather exceptional version of it here."

Lucy sighed and shook her head. How long could they talk about tea?

"You were telling me about your sister-in-law. That she was psychic?"

Lucy ears pricked up. She could have hugged Alec McKay.

"Indeed," Sir Jeffrey replied. "But Rosalie's unusual abilities, I'm afraid to say, brought her more than a fair share of heartache. She and my brother could never quite see eye to eye on her rather strange calling. I always tried to be open about it—to be sympathetic to how strongly Rosalie believed in those kinds of things—but Frederick refused to take any of it seriously. It was an embarrassment to him. But she often had visions of things that were about to occur, and with an accuracy that was, at times, quite uncanny. I'm a man of science, but I have encountered enough strange things over the years to suspect that there are forces at work on this planet that cannot always be explained away by logic or reason alone. Rosalie, I am convinced, could see into the future."

Lucy's heart fluttered.

"Was she able to ..."

Sir Jeffrey interrupted his guest. "I've probably said far too much about it already. I've never told a single soul in all these years. For Lucy's sake, I suppose." Sir Jeffrey paused. "But for some odd reason, I must admit that I suddenly feel compelled to speak about it. I have been sensing something in Lucy lately, something I have only ever seen in one other person—her dear mother."

Lucy couldn't believe what she was hearing. Her heart was pounding so hard and loud she feared it would block out the sound of her uncle's voice. She stood up from the bed and quietly tiptoed over to the wall, carefully pressing her ear against the cracked plaster.

"Could she—Rosalie, I mean—*really* see into the future?" Alec asked. "I promise you that our conversation will not go beyond this room."

Sir Jeffrey sighed, hesitating before he spoke again. "Sadly, I believe that she could. The night before their car accident, Rosalie had one of her more disturbing premonitions. She begged my brother to reconsider their travel plans, but it was to be an important evening for Frederick. A new business prospect had extended an invitation to attend a reception at his country estate in Kent. Frederick's position at his law firm would have been greatly enhanced if he and Rosalie could make a good impression and he was able to land the account. Cancelling was out of the question. Convincing her that her vision was nothing more than an overactive case of nerves, Frederick won out in the end and Rosalie reluctantly agreed to go. But alas, Mr. McKay, her intuitions proved to be deadly accurate."

"With all due respect to your brother's memory, I think I would have considered Rosalie's insights a rare gift, rather than something to be hidden away."

"Indeed, as I believe they should have, too," Sir Jeffrey continued. "But not everyone thinks as you and I do, Mr. McKay. Frederick had always relied strictly on logic to guide him through life. He never allowed himself to consider that there was more to the world than that which he could see with his own two eyes. Rosalie's abilities were nothing short of a burden to him, especially when people began to hear about her and seek her out for readings. Had he been less of a sceptic, then they might both be alive now. But he chose to view it as an annoyance instead. Abilities of this nature invariably bring a dose of sorrow and unhappiness, along with undue pressure and responsibility." For a moment, the room next door was silent. Then Lucy's uncle spoke again. "Are you familiar with the life of the great psychic Cheiro, Mr. McKay?"

"No. I don't think so."

"His real name was Count Louis Hamon, a man admired not only for his great charm and sensitivity, but for his intuitive ability to see into people's pasts and futures just by taking their hands into his and reading the lines upon them. Cheiro was a palmist by profession, and undoubtedly one of the best that ever lived. During the height of his career, between the early part of the twentieth century and up until his death in the late 1930s, he was the toast of Europe and the confidante of some of the most powerful men and women of the time—heads of state, the royal families of Britain and Russia, famous actors, poets, writers and musicians. Aside from making personal readings, 'the Count,' as he was also known, predicted world events with such detail and accuracy that no one could possibly have doubted his abilities. World wars, famines and plagues, assassinations, the fall of nations, the destruction of great cities and the loss of millions of lives—he foresaw them all. Would most people call this thing a gift, Mr. McKay? Perhaps not. Some might even consider it a curse. How must it have been, I have often wondered, to sense the tragic future of Nicholas II, Czar of Russia—as the Count reportedly did—and then reveal to the man that if he did not leave his home immediately, he and his beloved wife and children would perish at the hands of assassins?"

"And that's exactly what happened!"

"Indeed. Just as Count Louis had said it would. In those final days, living in fear of the Count's prediction but refusing to abandon his court, Nicholas gave instructions that a ship be kept at the ready, day and night, to whisk his family to safety at a moment's notice. But in the end, even the Czar of Russia could not prevent fate. Can you imagine how the man who foresaw these horrible events—and who tried in vain to prevent them—must have felt when news of the Russian royal family's slaughter reached him?"

"Pretty awful, I'd guess."

"And that is just one example of the power of his predictions. There were many, many others. You see, his strange ability was like a double-edged sword: both a blessing and a curse. Count Louis struggled with this gift throughout his entire life, but he could never escape it. The more famous he became, the more he was pursued by the masses, passing through such periods of mental strain and physical exhaustion that his own health was often seriously affected. But he never turned his back on his calling. In fact, toward the end of his life, he even attempted to educate those who were drawn to palmistry—the study of the hand—knowing that there may be other individuals struggling to understand and control the powers they had been granted. One 'student' of the Count's work was a young woman by the name of Lucinda Clarke. She was from one of the northern shires of England, born into a family of Romany gypsies—a people not altogether unfamiliar with the psychic world. Lucinda, however, was unusually gifted, even by *their* standards—"

"It's not a common name, is it? Lucinda, I mean?"

"It's a family name actually, passed down as I am sure you must have already guessed, to her great-great-granddaughter, Lucy Parnell."

Lucy, her ear still pressed against the wall, suddenly felt faint. Her hand instinctively wandered to the locket around her neck. She held onto it tight, as if the tiny picture inside it might somehow stop her from falling to the floor.

"And you think now that Lucinda may have passed more than just her name down to your niece."

"My sister-in-law firmly believed that she did. Of course, she never dared speak of it to Frederick. He would have been outraged by her suspicions. It was all nonsense to him, after all. But for some reason, Rosalie chose to confide in me. She recognized something different in the child right from the start, and was very concerned about how it might affect her later in life."

"Your sister-in-law noticed a family resemblance?"

"If that's what you could call it. Not long before she died, Rosalie told me that she sensed Lucy would be in grave danger one day because of her unusual talents. She made me promise, on my oath, that I would always look out for her. It's strange isn't it, that she would be compelled to ask *me*, a crusty old bachelor, such a thing? As if she knew, somehow that—"

"You would be raising her daughter one day?" Alec finished for him.

"Yes," Sir Jeffrey replied, "and because of that promise I made to Rosalie all those years ago, my devotion to Lucy is perhaps even stronger than it would normally have been."

"Does Lucy know anything about her family legacy?" Alec asked. "Or her mother's prediction?"

"I made a decision long ago that I would say nothing about it. I wanted to provide her with as normal an upbringing as I could under the circumstances and there was always the possibility, I supposed, that Rosalie might have been mistaken. But with everything that has been transpiring lately—with the arrival of this strange animal, Lucy's unusual bonding with it and now these visions she's been having—I am beginning to believe that Rosalie may have been right. It's been praying on my conscience all evening that I may have let Lucy down by not telling her everything, right from the beginning."

"I wouldn't feel too badly," Alec offered. "From what I've seen so far, Lucy seems to be a very intelligent and capable young lady. I have a feeling that she may figure it out all by herself soon enough. You were acting out of love and concern. And sometimes that's the best we can do for the ones we care about, isn't it? I'm sure Lucy wouldn't hold it against you."

Lucy lifted her ear away from the plaster wall and stood quietly for a few seconds. She didn't need to hear any more—there had been enough staggering news to digest for one day. But Alec McKay was right. She couldn't hold anything against her uncle. In fact, she felt sorry for him. It must have been a heavy burden for him to have shouldered all these years. At least now she understood why he had seemed so worried and preoccupied earlier and, more importantly, why she sometimes felt the strange things she did. The bizarre little experiences she'd had growing up—the haunting dreams, the flashes of insight, the weird tingles of déjà vu—all of those once disjointed pieces of her life had suddenly fallen into place.

Lucy slowly made her way back to the edge of her bed, sat down again and stared at the wall. She was not quite sure what any of this meant, but she did know that something important was happening around her. Something she had no control over was pulling her closer, inch by inch—to what end she couldn't begin to imagine. Feeling restless, she wandered over to the corner of the room where the animal enclosure rested on a table. She sat down in the wooden chair beside it, leaning forward and cradling her head in her hands. The creature was still sleeping, breathing in and out with soft chirping noises. Lucy tilted her head back, resting her neck against the hard top rung of the chair and her right hand on the table beside her. She closed her eyes and started to drift off, taking air into her lungs and blowing it out in time with the gentle rhythm of the creature's own breathing. She was almost asleep when the touch of something at the end of her hand jarred her eyes open. She held her breath, then slowly looked sideways. A long, slender lizard finger was wrapping itself around her thumb. She lifted her head and stared at the enclosure. The creature's eyes were open— bright emerald and glowing again—and Lucy immediately felt herself drawn in. They were irresistible and all-consuming and Lucy could sense—just as she had before—that the animal was trying to tell her something, trying to ask for her help. She felt such pity for him that she found herself reaching her other hand out toward the latch on the enclosure. She was about to turn it—until something stopped her. Other emotions suddenly swirled deep inside of her; thoughts she had never experienced before. Strange feelings of power and possession, as if she had just been granted the means to have anything she wanted. They were intoxicating, and she didn't want to let go of them, even though she knew she should.

Frightened and uncomfortable, Lucy quickly pulled her hand away. The long lizard finger reluctantly let go, then slowly slipped back through the bars. As the creature shuffled off to huddle in the far corner of the enclosure, Lucy stood up and headed for the door. Grasping the knob in her hand she turned it as quietly as she could, then tiptoed onto the landing. She felt groggy as she made her way down the stairs toward the kitchen, praying that a warm cup of tea might clear her head.

The sun had risen in the sky two times since she had last seen her mate, but the Other still could not calm the trembling in her body. She had heard him calling to her from the forest floor that first morning; warning her away. *Climb as high as you can,* he'd screeched, and his cries had sounded so frantic that she'd scrambled up the branches without looking back once. There she had stayed, too frightened to come down, hoping that she might soon hear him returning. But she had heard nothing as darkness came and went and came again, and the fear in her heart was becoming unbearable. She had not eaten or taken water since he'd left. Little birds had been flitting about for the last few hours, some even daring to alight on the branches next to her. They watched with curiosity, sensing her despair, finally realizing that the howls of the night jackal must have been true after all. Something was horribly wrong—one of the Golden Ones was really gone. Chirping and whistling, the forest birds fanned out through the trees, reaching Kathmandu before midday and stirring up the flocks of pigeons and sparrows that lived in the city parks and squares. Before nightfall, a thousand more birds had taken to the air, sweeping over the land like a huge tidal wave, spreading the distressing news from one body to the next—through every valley, canyon and forest, over deserts and mountains, across oceans and rivers and seas, barely stopping to rest until their message reached the ear of every other creature on earth.

8

THE HOLY MAN

THE DAWN OF A NEW DAY, Evan concluded upon rising the next morning, was probably the best time of all to take a stab at starting something over. In the hotel's small dining room, where an assortment of differently styled chairs surrounded a very long and uneven table, Evan looked over at Lucy and tried delivering a cheery *"Namaste"* as he sat down. She glanced up only briefly, then gave him a blank stare before she returned to the business of pushing another forkful of scrambled eggs around her plate.

"So what do you make of all this trouble, Sir Jeffrey?" Evan's father asked, peering over the edge of his newspaper.

"What trouble?"

"I guess you haven't seen the paper this morning then, eh?" he replied. "Take a look at this. I think you'll find it interesting." He folded the front section of the *Himalayan Times* in half and handed it across the table. "The hotel manager kindly offered me an English language newspaper along with my coffee this morning. I had noticed a few smaller items in the London news on the flight over, but I didn't think too much about it—until now, that is. It looks like the weird things they were talking about in England are starting to happen all over the place."

Sir Jeffrey unfolded the paper and began to study it. "Thank you, Mr. McKay. I've been so occupied with our animal since its arrival that I haven't had much time to think about anything el—" Sir Jeffrey stopped speaking, furrowing his brow as he continued reading. "Curious behaviour," he finally commented, turning the pages over. "Very curious, indeed."

"What is it?" Lucy shifted her chair closer to her uncle's so that she could see the newspaper, too.

"Reports of some unusual incidents in the natural world," he replied, pointing to one of the headlines.

"FROGS RAIN DOWN ALONG CALIFORNIA COAST," Lucy called out the headline as she began to read. "*Officials report that a series of small tornadoes may have been responsible for sweeping large clusters of frogs into the air and then depositing them over homes and businesses in towns along the coast, causing chaos for afternoon shoppers and commuters. There were no reports, however, of any tornadoes or even storm activity in the area at the time. 'It was like those creepy things were organized or something,' said Byron Everett, embattled mayor of one hamlet. 'Lined themselves up like little storm troopers and marched down Main Street like they knew what they were doing. And they were chomping away on everything they could get their little webbed feet on, too—chewed up all the flower floats for the Founder's Day parade tomorrow. And then, when they were finished, they just hopped away. Didn't catch a single one of them. And you can forget about all that crazy storm talk, too—wasn't a cloud in the sky.'*" Lucy looked up.

"I've heard about things like this happening before."

"As have I, my dear. But that's not all that's been going on, apparently." Sir Jeffrey pointed to another story, and then another. Lucy continued reading out the headlines.

"NORWEGIAN NAVY SUSPENDS SUBMARINE EXERCISES IN NORTH ATLANTIC—*Cites sonar interference from massive whale pods. Scientists at a loss to explain.* FAMED RINGLING BROTHERS CIRCUS CANCELS AUSTRALIAN TOUR—*Rumours rampant that animals are refusing to perform.* SEVERAL AIRPORTS IN EASTERN EUROPE FORCED TO SHUT DOWN—*Large flocks of birds continue to block airspace.* BRONX ZOO AND SEAWORLD IN FLORIDA FOLLOW OTHER ZOO CLOSURES IN BARCELONA, TORONTO AND MEXICO CITY—*Animals in hiding, keepers report; won't allow spectators.* CENTRAL PARK'S MOUNTED POLICE UNIT SIDELINED, AIRPORT SNIFFER DOGS TURN UP THEIR NOSES," Lucy stopped reading, amazed. "It just goes on and on!"

"Take a look at these other stories, my dear," he said, handing the pages over to Lucy. "There's quite a bit more."

"Like what?" Evan asked.

"Changes in traditional migratory flight routes, for one," Sir Jeffrey replied. "Flocks of birds and insects have been observed heading in entirely the wrong direction. This kind of sudden disruption in the distribution patterns of world wildlife is bound to have a significant impact on human interests. Can you imagine what would happen if the swarms of locusts heading one way suddenly changed direction and descended on some of the highest yielding farmland in the Midwest?"

"Economic disaster, I would imagine."

"Exactly, Mr. McKay. And then there are the large groups of animals that have been massing together in the oddest locations." He gestured toward the newspaper in Lucy's hands. "There's a report in there of a number of rail lines across Africa being brought to a standstill by herds of elephants, wildebeests and gazelles gathering on the tracks, not to mention domesticated animals refusing to do what we have always relied on them to do: providing milk, laying eggs, producing honey. It's as if they have all decided to become defiant—to mount some sort of gigantic, global protest. If it wasn't for the serious implications—the chaos and panic that it must be causing—it would be a simply fascinating opportunity to observe some never before seen behaviours. It's all quite extraordinary."

"So what do you think is going on?" Alec continued to flip through his portion of the paper, curious to see what else had been taking place.

"These types of things are known to happen occasionally, usually as isolated incidents. What's different this time, however, is the number of events and the extent of their range. These current episodes seem to be spread throughout the world and it appears that the scientific community is completely baffled. Each incident doesn't seem disruptive enough in itself to cause undue concern. But put all of them together at the same time, however, with widespread disruptions to travel, communication and trade, and the world may very soon find itself on its knees."

"But there must be some kind of reasonable explanation, right?"

"For something that can only be described as entirely *unreasonable*, Mr. McKay?" Sir Jeffrey asked, shaking his head. "It's possible, I suppose, though it would have to be something on a catastrophic scale to have had this type of global effect—a series of major earthquakes, perhaps, a direct hit or two from a large meteor storm, or some type of heightened underground volcanic activity. I don't believe that there have been any unusual geophysical changes in the past few days—at least none that have been reported. I can't imagine what else it could be. I'm sure, though, that theories are already circulating. Everyone will be throwing in their two cents, I imagine: global warming experts, seismologists, astronomers, environmentalists, even an astrologer or two with some planetary alignment theories. And, of course," he said, rolling his eyes, "the animal psychologist people will jump in on it, too."

"What about solar flares?" Evan asked. "We were talking about them in class a while ago and—"

"More likely to disrupt satellite communications and your cellphone signal," Sir Jeffrey replied. "But then again, Evan, your guess is as good as anyone else's." He took the newspaper from Lucy and laid it at the centre of the table. "What really worries me is that the news printed here is at least a day old. If these incidents are escalating, then there's no telling what might be happening out there right now."

Sir Jeffrey suddenly looked up.

"Did we happen to bring along that old transistor radio this time, Lucy?"

"Yes," she answered. "It's in my room. I was listening to some music the other night."

"Gee, let me guess," Evan remarked. "Polkas or waltzes?"

"As a matter of fact, it was Strauss," Lucy replied, delighted at Evan's interest in her musical tastes—until she noticed that he was smirking. She left the room in a huff.

"What can you get on a thing like that?" Alec asked. "Voice of America?"

"From time to time, although BBC World Service is slightly more reliable."

When Lucy returned with the transistor, Sir Jeffrey immediately began fiddling with the tuning knob, attempting to find a signal. He was about to give up when the intermittent bursts of static finally gave way to the clipped voice of a BBC announcer.

"... and that situation is estimated to be costing millions of dollars a day, amidst new reports of the widespread blockage of major cargo routes by thousands of sea mammals. Stay tuned in the next hour for an up-to-date investigation on how the shipping industry is planning to deal with these crushing losses. In Geneva this weekend, the world's top scientists are gathering for an emergency meeting. The hope is that by sharing information, they might be able to determine exactly what is happening to global ecosystems and why. And this just in ... we have unconfirmed reports from our affiliate in Boston that Logan International Airport has been shut down due to an unspecified threat. It is believed that no flights are being allowed to leave or enter the city ..."

There was silence then as the radio went dead. Sir Jeffrey tried twisting the knob again, but to no avail. There was nothing to hear now: no static, no sound at all.

"It appears that one of our best links to the outside world has been cut off," he sighed.

"Do you think this might be some kind of warning?" Lucy suggested.

"What do you mean, my dear?"

"Well, strange animal activity has been observed and documented for centuries in other civilizations—the Chinese, Greeks, Romans and Egyptians—correct? People back then were much more in tune with the powers of the natural world than we are. They were more respectful of it. They believed that animals were intuitive and that they possessed the ability to predict catastrophes before they happened. They didn't feel foolish at all in heeding these warnings. In fact, it was quite acceptable." Lucy stopped talking for a moment and looked around the table. Her uncle and Alec McKay were staring at her with obvious interest. Evan, for his part, looked as if he was trying to stifle a laugh. Idiot, she thought. She wasn't about to let him dictate what she would or wouldn't say. She took a deep breath and continued with her theory. "Even we know that animals often act strangely before storms and earthquakes, but we've never paid any solid scientific attention to this phenomenon. I know there are some people around doing research—like trying to predict earthquakes by documenting animal behaviour in the days leading up to them—but it's not been given that much credence yet. Maybe it's not that something catastrophic *has* happened on the earth. Maybe it's about to. Maybe something's wrong out there and these animals are warning us."

Waiting for her uncle's reaction, Lucy noticed the look that passed between Sir Jeffrey and Alec. Evan's father spoke first.

"Do you have a particularly strong feeling about this, Lucy?" he turned and asked.

"Um ... I'm not sure what you mean, Mr McKay," she replied, hesitating. "It was just an idea ..."

Lucy lowered her head and started playing with her fork

again. She knew exactly what Alec McKay meant, but she didn't want to let on. She was determined not to let her uncle know that she had overheard his conversation the night before—at least not until she discovered more about it herself. She felt confused and vulnerable, but took a deep breath instead, then looked up and tried to smile as confidently as possible.

"Maybe it's just the end of the whole damned world," Francis Darby mumbled gruffly as he entered the dining room from the hallway.

Lucy immediately stopped smiling and stared down at the table. The change, Evan noticed, was remarkable. A minute ago she'd been lecturing them like a professor, now she seemed distressed that there wasn't much food left on her plate to play with. He watched her discreetly out of the corner of his eye. She looked at her plate, out the window, at the newspaper—anywhere but directly at the man who'd just sat down opposite her. But Francis Darby, Evan noticed, didn't seem to want to look anywhere but right at Lucy.

"An interesting observation, Mr. Darby," Sir Jeffrey remarked dryly, scanning now through the last section of newspaper, "though a bit fatalistic one, wouldn't you say?"

Darby grunted. He reached toward the big platter at the centre of the table and grabbed a piece of toast.

The conversation around the table grew noticeably quieter. As Sir Jeffrey gruffly made the introductions—this Darby was apparently the field assistant—Evan decided to give it one last try with Lucy.

"So what do you do for fun around here, anyway?" he asked her, laying his knife and fork across the top of his plate and pushing it all away. "When you're not busy listening to

Strauss or taking care of your important scientific work, I mean."

"Fun?" Lucy replied, looking blankly at him again.

"You know ... *fun*," Evan replied, staring back at her in disbelief. "Entertainment ... recreation ... good times?"

"What?" Lucy replied vaguely. "Oh, *that*. Well, there are my books, of course, and ..."

"*Fun* may be alright for some," Francis Darby interrupted, taking a large bite of toast, "but some of us still have important work to do around here. Isn't that so, Sir Jeffrey?"

"Perhaps you can show our visitor the market square, Lucy," Sir Jeffrey said, completely ignoring Darby's comments. He wiped a drying drip of egg yolk off his chin with his napkin as he spoke. "They have a fascinating collection of things, I've been told—quite a large variety of handcrafts and local food items. I'm sure you'll find something of interest."

Darby, an expression of annoyance of his face, took a large mouthful of coffee, then noisily pushed his chair away from the table and stood up.

"Leaving us so soon, Mr. Darby?" Sir Jeffrey asked.

Darby nodded. "There are a still a few things I have to take care of."

"I do hope that one of them might be sending that man of yours over so that I can take a look his wounds," Sir Jeffrey continued. "Perhaps he was mistaken about the source of his injury. It may have been another animal that clawed him— something poisonous, perhaps. It would be wise to have him properly examined."

"I already told you that I dismissed him," Darby replied sternly, his eyes flashing around the table until they landed directly on Lucy again. "Remember?"

"Oh, yes, that's right, isn't it?" Sir Jeffrey replied. "Well, if by chance he's still in the area somewhere, perhaps you can seek him out and tell him I'd like a word."

"I doubt that's possible," Darby snapped. "I'll wager he's a thousand miles from here."

Lucy looked up and stared straight at him. She opened her mouth to speak, but the icy expression on Darby's faced stopped her dead. Evan stared, fascinated. What was going on?

"Well, see what you can do," Sir Jeffrey replied.

As he walked out of the room, Darby crushed his table napkin into a tight ball and tossed it at the young girl who had been serving the coffee. She tried to catch it before it fell to the floor, upsetting the dishes she was struggling to carry. Evan leaned down and picked up the napkin, laying it gently on the top of the dish pile. She smiled shyly at him.

"That market thing sounds pretty good," Evan said, popping his head up again and grinning at Lucy. He suspected that Lucy was far from pleased with her uncle's suggestion about an outing, but he wasn't giving up just yet. The girl *was* downright insufferable, that much he knew. However, she was his only hope if he wanted to explore. She could show him where to go and what to do. And besides, annoying her was just too easy—and too much fun.

"I think I'd really like to go to a place like that," he continued, still smiling. "Sounds like a lot of fun. But only if it's okay with my dad—I promised to help him set up his camera equipment."

Alec, leaning over his camera bags now, grunted at him from the other side of the room. "Don't need you just yet, son. That bus ride in from Kathmandu gave some of the equipment a bit of a beating. It's going to take me a while to sort everything out. I'll stay here. You kids go on and have a good time. You can give me a hand setting things up later."

"It's settled then, Lucy. You and Evan shall go," Sir Jeffrey replied. "That's excellent, isn't it?"

"Yes, Uncle Jeff," she responded flatly. "Just wonderful." She stood up and trailed past Evan's chair without looking at him. "Come on then," she sighed from the doorway, "if you *really* want to go that much."

"You're in for a special treat, young man!" said Sir Jeffrey, patting Evan on the back as he stood up to leave. "We'll see you both later for dinner, alright?" He called after his niece. "Six o'clock, Lucy?"

"Yes, fine."

Evan followed Lucy out into the lobby.

"Can I get my jacket first?" he asked.

"Doesn't matter to me," she replied. "I don't see why you'd want it, though. It's probably already too warm."

Evan hesitated. He never went anywhere without his jacket, and he wasn't about to start now. "Just wait for me, okay? I'll be right back."

Evan raced up the stairs two at a time and bolted into his room, grabbing the jacket he'd tossed at the foot of his bed. He unzipped the right inner pocket, reaching his fingers all the way inside. The essential items were still there: his wallet, a comb, a pen, a pair of sunglasses, a clean but crumpled clump of Kleenex, and the small box of waterproof matches he'd never used but always carried with him—ever since the day he'd gotten lost by himself in the woods for four hours at Scout camp. That was more than six years ago. He slipped the jacket on, but it seemed uncomfortable somehow, and lopsided. He reached into his luggage and retrieved Jack

Trenton's old tour guide, shoving it into the inside left pocket to provide some ballast. That felt better. The thing had to be good for something. He grinned to himself. This could turn out to be the most fun he'd had in days. So far, his ability to irritate Lucy Parnell was right on the mark. He made his way back down the stairs, jumping them three at a time, then flung the hotel's front door wide open, almost knocking Lucy off the top step. She stumbled awkwardly down the rest of them, shooting him a look that was becoming very familiar. Then she started walking so fast down the street that he had to sprint to keep up.

"Hey, wait up!" he shouted, wishing with every leap forward that he hadn't insisted on bringing his jacket along. The sweat was already starting to break out on his forehead. But there was no way he was taking it off yet: not when it was a matter of saving face.

"So, you're from Canada, are you?" Lucy asked, after he'd finally caught up.

"Yep," he panted.

"Lovely country."

"Guess so," Evan grunted.

"Too bad they don't teach people any manners back there, eh, McKay?" she remarked.

"What's that supposed to mean?" he shot back. "And the name's Evan, by the way."

"Come on now, McKay," Lucy continued, completely ignoring his comments. "Surely you haven't forgotten how rude you were last night."

Evan flinched. "Oh ... *that*. I couldn't help it, I guess. We'd just gotten off that stupid bus and I was feeling really tired and kind of sick, too. Besides, haven't you ever done anything like that before? Laughed when you shouldn't have?"

"No, I don't believe that I have," she replied sternly. "And if I ever did, the very least I would do is apologize. Immediately."

"Oh," he replied, shrugging his shoulders. "Then I'm *sorry*, I guess."

"There. That wasn't so hard, was it?" she said. "Better late than never, I suppose."

"Well, you're not the easiest person to apologize to, you know," Evan remarked, still trying to catch his breath. "I might not have said the word 'sorry,' but I did try to make it up to you. You didn't even notice, did you? And you can be pretty rude yourself—trying to insult people. Or hasn't anyone ever told you that before?"

Lucy stopped walking. She turned, folded her arms in front of her and stared straight at him, tapping her foot on the ground.

"Alright, McKay," she sighed. "This isn't getting either of us anywhere. It looks like we're going to be stuck with each other for a while. How about we say we're even? Equally rude?"

"Fine by me."

Lucy started walking again, and Evan followed. For awhile, neither of them spoke. They made their way along dusty streets, past rows of stone buildings and thin, dark alleyways. The mid-morning sun was hot and glaring. Evan pulled the sunglasses out of his jacket.

"The truth is you looked like a complete idiot," he suddenly blurted, popping the glasses on, "sitting flat out in the hallway like that. Anyone would have laughed. I think I even saw your uncle trying to hide a smile."

"That's preposterous!" Lucy shouted. "He'd never do a thing like that!"

Evan held up his hands in defence. "I'm just telling you what I saw ..."

Lucy glared at him out of the corner of her eye. "Are you teasing me now, McKay?"

Evan shrugged again. "Maybe."

"Truce?" she asked, a thin smile forming on her lips.

"Okay," he replied. "Truce."

"Did I really look that bad?"

"Absolutely ridiculous," he replied.

Lucy cringed.

"But your recovery wasn't bad," he added quickly.

"Thanks," she murmured. "I think."

"So where is this market, anyway?" Evan asked, relieved to be finally changing the subject. "Is it far away?"

"It's just around this next corner." Lucy sighed.

"And what are those monkeys doing over there?"

"My goodness, McKay, you're suddenly just full of questions, aren't you?" Lucy glanced across the street. "What monkeys? I've never noticed any around here before."

"Well, you can't *really* miss them," said Evan, pointing to an area across the street where a bit of a commotion had broken out. "They're the ones running up and down the buildings over there and pelting people with fruit."

"Oh," Lucy replied. A furrow of concern creased her forehead. "That's very odd, isn't it? I wonder if it has anything to do with those newspaper re—" All at once, Lucy stopped speaking. She lunged sideways, darting quickly into a doorway.

"What's going—?"

"Ssshh!" she whispered, grabbing Evan's sleeve and

pulling him in after her. His body bumped painfully against the rough stone wall at the side of the doorframe.

"Hey! What gives?" Evan cried, rubbing at his shoulder. "Are the monkeys heading this way or something?"

"No! It's Francis Darby!" she replied. "Over there!" She pointed to a man across the street, leaning his body against a stone archway. He was watching the antics of the monkeys with an expression of mild amusement.

"That guy at breakfast? The one who works for your uncle?"

"Yes," Lucy whispered.

Evan raised his eyebrows. "And we have to hide from him because ..."

"I don't trust him."

"He was the one who found the animal, right?"

"Yes." Lucy replied. "He claims that he ..."

"What?"

"Nothing."

"Come on—tell me. You dragged me off the street and into this doorway. You practically dislocated my shoulder, too. The least you can do is let me in on why we're hiding from this guy."

Lucy turned then and stared into Evan's eyes. Her gaze was so intent, so piercing, that he started to feel uncomfortable.

"Stop staring at me like that," he protested, screwing up his face. "What's up with you, anyway? Don't you think you can trust me, either?"

"No, that's not it ..." she began again slowly, still staring. "I guess you're alright." She paused for a second. "Francis Darby, however, is another story."

"He's made a pass at you, hasn't he?" Evan grinned

knowingly, blurting the words out with such bluntness that they seemed to catch Lucy completely off guard. She looked down at her feet, trying to hide the blush that was spreading across her face.

"NO! And why would you say an awful thing like that?" she protested.

"Come on!" Evan responded. "You'd have to be blind, or completely dense, not to see it. You *must* have you noticed the way he looks at you. At breakfast this morning, he was practically—"

"Yes! Yes! Okay!" Lucy groaned, trying to stop him from saying more. "Do you think anyone else noticed?" she asked nervously.

"Like who?" Evan replied. "You mean your uncle, right?" He shook his head. "I doubt it. No disrespect or anything, but he seems a little clued out."

"About almost everything but his work," Lucy sighed. "He's my uncle and I love him very much, but he's always been that way, you know. In this case, it's probably a good thing, I suppose."

"Yeah? Why's that?"

Lucy hesitated. She stared back into Evan's eyes. He could see her struggling with something, trying to decide whether to confide in him or not. Given his earlier behaviour, Evan realized that she had absolutely no reason to trust him. All at once, however, he found himself hoping that she would.

"Well ..." she began slowly, "there's something off about Darby's story. He said he found the animal living high up in the mountains, beyond the Tibetan border. But that doesn't really fit."

"Why not?"

"It isn't physically equipped to live in a climate that extreme," she replied. "At least, it doesn't appear to be. There are other places, at much lower elevations, where it's more likely to have come from. But the animals there are protected by law and the capture or killing of them is forbidden. When I questioned Darby about it, he became very annoyed. Then it started to seem as if he were threatening me, or rather, my uncle."

"Seriously?" Evan asked. "Like how?"

"Well, he went on and on about how dangerous and unpredictable this place could be."

"Well, I can't argue with that," Evan replied, remembering his bus ride and the passages he'd read in Trenton's journal.

"But then he suggested that Uncle Jeff might come to some sort of harm," Lucy continued. "I think he meant if I stirred things up or asked too many questions." She poked her head out from the doorway then, scanning the street for any sign of Darby. "And then there's the whole business with Tyrone."

"Tyrone?"

"One of Darby's men." Lucy took a tentative step onto the street, looking left and right. "He didn't come back from the expedition with the rest of the men. Apparently he was badly scratched by the animal, or so Darby claimed. But when Uncle Jeff wanted to examine Tyrone's wounds, Darby said he'd sent him packing—for insubordination or something."

"Convenient," Evan remarked.

"Except that I've seen him—right here in Dhunche! And

he looked like he'd had a proper beating, too." She took one last look up and down the street. "I think the coast is clear," she said. "Come on, let's get out of here. You still want to see the market, don't you?"

"Wait!" Evan put his hand on her arm. "Maybe we should head back to the hotel right now and tell your uncle about all of this. And we could tell my dad, too. He might be able to help."

"Are you joking? I can't tell my uncle about any of this!" she protested. "About the way Darby's been acting with me, or the threats or Tyrone. Uncle Jeff would definitely fire him right away and I can't risk that. I'd never forgive myself if anything happened to him. Promise me you won't tell your father, either. He'd just feel that he had to say something, or worse—do something. Okay?"

"I don't know if that's such a good—"

"Promise me?" she asked again, squeezing his arm.

"Alright, alright," he replied. "If you think it's that important. But what are you going to do, then?"

"I'm going straight to the top," she replied, pulling Evan out of the doorway. She started walking down the street. "When Melville Carew gets here, I'm going to tell him all about it. He was supposed to be here already. Something must have delayed him ..."

"Carew?" Evan interrupted, rolling his eyes. "Ah, come on, Lucy. He sounds like a complete nut!"

"How would you know?"

"Your uncle told me and my dad about him. Some weird stuff he read in an article."

"I read that story, too," Lucy replied. "But just because he's a little eccentric, that's no reason to—"

"A *little* eccentric!" Evan exclaimed, grimacing. "Like making mummies and freezing people's heads?"

Lucy sighed. "I know, I know. It sounds ridiculous. But I really need to confide in someone about all of this, McKay—someone who can actually do something. And Melville Carew might be the only one with enough clout to take care of a person like Francis Darby. I need some help."

"Well, *I* could help you, I guess," Evan suggested. "If this Carew guy doesn't turn up, that is."

"You?" she replied, chuckling.

"What? That seems funny to you or something?"

"Be serious, McKay. You hate this place, right? I'll bet you don't want to be here at all."

"That doesn't mean I couldn't help, does it?" he replied. "I'm not completely useless, you know."

Lucy stopped walking. She tilted her head at him and stared. "What's this all about? Is there an adventurer lurking deep down inside you somewhere? Is that what you're trying to say?"

"I don't know," he answered, shrugging. "Maybe."

"Well, trust me, McKay," she sighed as they started walking again. "You have no idea what you might be getting into. It could get pretty dangerous."

"I may not be a world traveller like you," Evan replied, offended, "but that doesn't mean I'm a coward!"

"I never said that you were," Lucy replied, raising her voice. "I'm SORRY."

"Oh, so you're going to rub it in, eh?"

"Rub *what* in?"

"That whole thing from before—about saying 'sorry.'"

Lucy threw up her hands in frustration. "You're hopeless,

McKay," she sighed. "Besides, I thought we'd declared a truce."

"That only works if everybody honours it."

"Fine! Can we start over again, then?" she groaned, looking around. "Anyway, we're here—at the market. Isn't that what you wanted in the first place?"

Lucy marched forward—past the racks of brightly woven shawls, Tibetan jackets and rows of bamboo flutes and tea bowls—stopping in front of the third stall to her right, where an elderly couple were selling carpets. Lucy smiled at the old woman as she picked up the edge of one of the more colourful pieces on display.

"Nice," Evan commented, slowly running his fingertips along the fringe at the opposite end.

"Yes, very," Lucy replied. She lifted her head and glanced down the street to where the food vendors were setting out their wares. "You hungry, McKay?" she asked, a sly smile on her lips. "It's been a while since breakfast. Or are you *still* feeling a little sick from all the travelling?"

There was no reply. Lucy glanced at Evan, expecting to find an unpleasant expression on his face. Instead, he was staring intently in another direction.

"Who's that man over there?" he asked, tipping his head sideways as he whispered into Lucy's ear.

She slowly turned to take a look. The man wore a bright yellow tunic that was soiled and torn in several places. His grey hair hung about his face in thick, matted strands, but his eyes were vibrant and piercing and full of life—and completely fixed on her.

"Do you know him or something?" Evan continued. "He's staring right at you."

"He's a sadhu," Lucy replied. "A Hindu holy man. And I'm not sure why he's staring, actually."

"Sadhu?"

"They live on the streets, like beggars," Lucy explained. "They're supposed to give up all the pleasures of an earthly life to find their way to spiritual enlightenment. They survive on the charity of others."

"Well, he's still staring and I think he's coming over here now."

"Relax, McKay. I don't imagine he's going to hurt us. He's a holy man. He's pledged himself to a life of peaceful existence, right? I wouldn't be scared of him."

"Why do you keep thinking I'm scared of everything?" Evan replied, sounding annoyed. "I was just asking about him, that's all!"

As he approached, the mysterious man began to remove a long garland of orange marigolds from around his neck. When he reached the street corner where Lucy and Evan were standing, he leaned toward her, slipping the colourful strand around her neck.

"What's he doing that for?" Evan whispered.

"I'm not sure." Lucy whispered back.

"Maybe he's paying you a compliment or something," Evan suggested.

"I highly doubt that, McKay" she said drolly. But when she smiled and nodded her head at the man, his dark eyes sparkled even brighter.

"Um ... thank you," she stammered. She lifted the string of bright flower heads up to her nose and sniffed. "They're very beautiful." She bowed to him. "*Namaste.*"

The man murmured something back at her and nodded.

Then he stood and stared.

"What's he doing now?" Evan whispered, impatiently nudging Lucy in her side. "Why's he still staring?"

"I don't know!" she shot back sharply. "Be *quiet* for a second, will you? I think he wants to tell me something."

Suddenly, the man crouched down in the street, reaching out for a twig that was lying near his hand. He moved it around slowly, making a series of long sweeping marks in the sand.

"Well, I hope you can read Hindi or Nepali," Evan sighed, "or whatever that is."

"It's not writing," Lucy replied. "I think it's a map."

"Huh?"

"See? He's drawn a big mountain range there," she pointed, "and a village over here. Those are buildings. Can't you tell?"

Evan squinted his eyes, then shrugged his shoulders. "Whatever you say, Lucy. But it doesn't look like anything to me."

"Quick! Do you have a pen on you?" she suddenly blurted. "Or a pencil ... anything!"

"Um, no ... yeah ... wait—I do." Evan shoved his hands inside his jacket and rooted around. Finally he pulled out an old blue ballpoint pen, its transparent plastic barrel almost empty of ink.

Lucy grabbed at it. "Great! And some paper?"

"What?" Evan exclaimed. "That, too? I don't usually carry piles of paper around on me, you know."

"Anything, McKay! A map, or a postcard, or ..."

"How about an old guidebook?" Evan announced with satisfaction, suddenly remembering what he had stuffed into the inside lining of his jacket earlier. He pulled Jack Trenton's book out and, with a smug smile, waved it about in Lucy's face. She reached up and grabbed it right out of his hands.

"Perfect!" she replied. She flipped through the book, stopping at one of the blank pages at the back. "We'd better get this stuff down before the wind blows it away," she said, crouching down next to the sadhu. "Look. I think he's drawing some sort of pathway now—a route, or something." She looked up and grinned at Evan. "By the way—thanks. You know, McKay, you've actually turned out to be quite a useful person to have around."

Evan shrugged again. "Gee, thanks a lot," he replied, rolling his eyes. "I think."

Lucy gripped the pen and began to draw. As she had predicted, the wind that was swirling through the marketplace had started to erode the crude map almost as quickly as she could copy it down.

"There. Done!" she exclaimed, standing up again. "And just in time, too. The wind's already blown most of it away."

"Seems to have blown that old holy guy away, too," Evan exclaimed, looking up.

"What?" Lucy spun around, her eyes searching every corner of the market. The sadhu had vanished—as quickly and silently as the map he'd drawn in the sand.

"What was *that* all about?" Evan asked.

Lucy, flipping through the rest of the guidebook now, absently shook her head.

"I don't know." She began walking forward into the street, still staring down at the book. "What is this thing, anyway?"

"It's an old guidebook to Nepal. From the sixties. I was reading it on the bus. Some guy gave it to my ... LUCY!"

Evan reached forward, grabbing a handful of Lucy's thin cotton shirt in his hand. He pulled her back toward him, wrapping both of his arms tightly around her waist. Inches away, a speeding bicycle swerved to miss her. The rider shook his fist in the air as he shot past, shouting something at them in Nepali.

"What's wrong with you?" Evan panted, his heart pounding in his throat. "You really should watch where you're going, for Pete's sake! You're going to get yourself killed!"

Lucy took a few deep breaths before she spoke. "See? I was right, McKay. You really are rather useful to have around, aren't you?"

Lucy was standing completely still now, trembling a little. Evan's arms weren't budging. She couldn't help but think of Francis Darby just then and how it had felt to have his arms wrapped around her this way. She shuddered as she remembered her desperation to wriggle out of them as fast as she could. But this felt very different. She didn't feel like pulling away this time. In fact, she didn't mind it at all.

9

THE LONGING

EVAN CLEARED HIS THROAT and let his arms fall to his sides. Looking straight ahead and still clutching the guidebook, Lucy slowly made her way to a low stone wall at the street corner and leaned her back against it. She felt too flustered and embarrassed to even imagining looking Evan in the eye.

"Have you read through this thing?" she mumbled, glancing down at the book again.

"What do you think?" he replied drolly. "You ever been on that bus from Kathmandu?"

Lucy nodded. "I remember *that* all too well. I think I would have read the entire Kathmandu telephone book, if it would have made the time pass any faster." Lucy continued browsing through the pages. "But *this* is very interesting. Who's Jack Trenton?" she asked, noting the inscription at the front.

"The brother of some guy my father knows back at his London office," Evan replied. "He wrote the notes along the margins and drew the sketches, too. Some of them aren't that

129

bad, either—except for the one of the Abominable Snowman. That looks a little cheesy, if you ask me. I mean, not that I've ever seen one myself or anything—"

"Abominable Snowman?" Lucy interrupted with excitement. "Really? He drew a *cryptid*?"

"A what?"

"A cryptid," she repeated. "It means hidden creature. Although the word is often used these days to describe something more mysterious—a being with mythical connotations, some would even say supernatural."

"Well, Trenton drew his sketch right after he saw one," Evan replied, taking the book from her. "That's what he said, anyway. Here, I'll show you. It's about three-quarters of the way through." Evan flipped through the pages until he found Jack Trenton's sketch and the accompanying notes about his terrifying encounter on the mountainside. "See?" Evan pointed his finger as he placed the book back in Lucy's hands. "There it is."

Lucy began to read Trenton's accounts.

"It's pretty neat actually," Evan offered. "Afterward he felt really weird about the whole thing. He tried over and over to find what he'd seen again. Finally, he ended up at this Buddhist monastery and—"

"Sshhh!" Lucy glanced up at him, a look of annoyance on her face. "Be quiet! I'm trying to read it for myself, McKay!"

Evan clenched his jaw and turned away. How could anyone be so annoying? He focused his attention on the market again, half hoping to see the holy man—what had Lucy called him? The sadhu—again. The stalls were busier now, the local residents no doubt shopping for their daily supplies. The smells from the food stalls were becoming more and more appetizing as the morning wore on. Maybe he was hungry, after all. He took a deep breath. Okay. He'd swallow his pride and ask Lucy if she was hungry. Maybe he could get them a bite to eat while she finished reading. When he turned back to speak to her, however, Evan noticed that the expression on Lucy's face had totally changed. At first she'd looked intrigued by what she was reading. Now she seemed more than just a little troubled. She turned her face away from the book and stared into the street.

"What is it?" he asked. "What's the matter?"

"I'm not sure, really."

"Well, what did he write there, then?" Evan asked, straining his neck to see over her shoulder.

"It's more of a feeling I have, not anything he actually wrote," Lucy replied, hesitating.

"A *feeling* about ...?"

"About the animal that's been captured ... and the power it possesses."

"You mean *our* little animal back at the hotel?" Evan asked. "What, like it's an Abominable Snowman or something? What is it called again? A cryptoid?"

"Cryp*tid*," she sighed. "And no, not like that, exactly. Something similar, I suppose. But maybe even more powerful." As Lucy stared down at the book in her hands, Evan could see them trembling. "I need to know more about this, McKay," she continued. "I have to know. But Jack Trenton doesn't say all that much, does he? His thoughts sort of drift away a bit, right up until he stops writing completely."

"Maybe he just ran out of things to say," Evan suggested.

Lucy shrugged her shoulders.

"Or maybe he found the answers he was looking for,"

Evan continued.

"And he just didn't feel the need to ramble on about it in some old notes any more?" she added.

"Maybe," Evan suggested.

"Where's the sadhu's map?" she mumbled to herself, turning the pages one by one. "I need to look at it again. Um ... there it is," she remarked. "No ... wait a minute." She quickly flipped forward to another page and then back again. "That's not *mine*. Mine's further at the back. This is another map. It's done in black pen—Jack Trenton's black pen, not blue like mine. But it's almost exactly the same!" Lucy shoved the book under Evan's nose. "See?"

Evan slowly nodded his head, trying to compare the two maps as Lucy began pacing in front of him.

"What do you think it means?" he asked.

"Well, it's obviously a map to somewhere Jack Trenton had been," Lucy replied, "or somewhere he was planning to go, right?"

"Like the monastery?"

"Could be," Lucy replied. "But the sadhu at the market drew it for me, too." She stopped pacing and stared at Evan. The puzzled look was back in her eyes. "But why? Why *me*? And what was he trying to tell me when he said, 'seek the one who lives beyond the clouds'?"

Evan stared at Lucy for a moment, trying to decide how to answer. When in doubt, he figured, tell the truth.

"He didn't say that, Lucy."

"Yes, he *did*," she replied adamantly. "In English, oddly. He said it while he was drawing out the map. Come on! You must have heard it!"

"I didn't hear anything."

"You didn't? But I was sure that I ..." Lucy face turned ashen as she once again leaned on the wall. She pushed a stray piece of hair off her face. Noise from the market drifted over to where they stood, filling the temporary silence. "We should go there," she said suddenly, "to where the map says. It *must* be important. And if it turns out to be the place where Jack Trenton found the answers to the things that were troubling him, then maybe we'll find our answers there, too."

Evan sighed. *"Our* answers? You mean *your* answers. Be honest, at least. It's you who's troubled by something. Not me."

"You're not just a tiny bit curious about all of this, McKay?" she shot back, clearly agitated now. "I would have thought that there were *some* things you'd like to know. Like why Trenton was so upset and why he needed to find peace from his own thoughts, and why ..." Lucy stopped speaking. She rubbed her hands over her face and groaned.

"Are you okay?"

She shook her head. "I'm not sure."

"Come on, Lucy," Evan spoke softly, trying as best he could to calm her down. "You're not really serious about going all the way to this monastery, are you? It's got to be hours and hours away ... or days even ..."

"I couldn't be more serious about anything, McKay. I just have a feeling about it. A feeling that all of this—everything that's been going on around here—is somehow linked to the animal. Our animal—to its capture and imprisonment." She looked straight into Evan's eyes then and whispered. "Maybe even to everything that's happening out in the world, too. When Uncle Jeff showed me the paper at breakfast this morning, I felt it right away. An instant connection to something bigger. I got goosebumps all over."

"Really?" Evan asked, grinning. "Well, I did notice you acting a little strangely, but I figured it was because of the way Darby was drooling all over you."

She glared at him. "I should hit you for that, you know."

"Sorry."

"Just think about it," she said, calmer now. "When did all of those things first start happening? When Darby made the capture!"

"It's probably just coincidence, Lucy. Stuff like that happens sometimes."

"It could be," she replied. "But I don't think so." She paused and took another deep breath, as if the next words weren't going to come easily. "Come with me," she mumbled softly. "I really don't want to go by myself."

Evan stared at her, speechless. If she was desperate enough to ask for his help—after all of the tension and arguments—she must be serious.

"But you're going to go anyway, right?" he remarked coolly. "Whether I agree to go or not?"

"Probably."

Evan looked off at the distant mountains and sighed. He distinctly remembered telling his dad that he didn't want to go trekking in Nepal. "Well, I guess I'm going too, then."

Lucy stepped forward with open arms. If she had thought to hug him just then, she changed her mind. She quickly lowered her hands and clapped them together in triumph, instead.

"I knew you wouldn't let me down!" she blurted, a little awkwardly. "See? There really *is* an adventurer lurking deep down inside you." She grinned at him. "Thanks, Evan."

He shrugged. "Hey! Thanks yourself."

"For what?"

"For *finally* calling me Evan."

Lucy smiled again. "Well, it's just seemed like the right time, I suppose. I can't keep on calling you McKay now, can I? It sounds sort of impersonal. After all, you've saved my life once already."

"I said I'll go, okay?" Evan replied sternly. "Just as long as you promise I'll never have to do that again."

"Okay, okay. I promise." She opened the book up again with excitement. *"There's a one-eyed yellow idol to the north of Khatmandu,"* she read, squinting at the very small handwriting. "That's odd. Trenton wrote this poem out, too?"

"Yeah. You ever heard of it?"

"Better than that. I had to memorize the whole thing for school once," Lucy replied. "All eleven verses. Old John Milton Hayes would probably roll over in his grave if he knew how many times that piece of his had been recited in the past hundred years or so. He was a soldier in the British army, you know."

"He was?" Evan remarked. "Hey, just like old Mad Carew, eh?"

"I suppose so," Lucy replied. "He was a bit of a mystery man, too. Not that much is known about him, except that he was a soldier and an actor of some sort. He didn't write too many poems, either—just a handful."

Evan peered over Lucy's shoulder again. "He spelled Kathmandu wrong."

"It was just the way they sometimes did it back then."

"Oh," Evan replied. "I never did get the chance to finish reading the whole thing. How does it end, anyway?"

"Well, Mad Carew is in love with the colonel's daughter,

right?" Lucy began. "He wants to give her a present for her birthday. She tells him that the only thing she wants is the green jewel that's set into the face of a local statue—a sacred golden statue."

"The green eye of the yellow god?" Evan asked.

"Precisely," Lucy replied. "Everyone's knows that it would be very dangerous and very foolish to take something as revered and holy as that, but the colonel's daughter is just having some fun with poor old Mad Carew—teasing him on a bit. What she doesn't know is that he's so crazy about her that he's likely to do anything to please her. He disappears one night and is found later, staggering back to the barracks, his forehead bleeding, his uniform torn. She rushes to his side and he tells her to look in his pocket, where she discovers the jewel—the green eye of the golden statue. She doesn't *really* want it now, so she leaves him there with it, only to return later to find him dead—a knife through his heart. She is horrified, of course. He had done the unthinkable for her—offended the gods—and now he has paid the price. And who knows? His soul has probably been damned for all eternity, too, or something like that. And she's left behind in her guilt to tend his grave," Lucy sighed, staring straight ahead. Her head was tilted slightly to one side, as if something important had just occurred to her. "End of poem," she slowly whispered.

"Wow. So what do you think it all means?" Evan asked.

"What? The poem?" Lucy asked. "Or the reason Jack Trenton felt haunted enough to write it all down?"

"Umm ... I'm not really sure. Both?"

"Maybe it's about the same thing," she murmured, her eyes still staring ahead.

"Huh?"

"Couldn't it all be about obsession? An insatiable desire to have something or take something that doesn't belong to you—shouldn't belong to you? A poet soldier wrote about it, nearly a hundred years ago. Then Jack Trenton experienced the same feelings up on that mountainside. And the weird thing is I think I know exactly how he felt ..." Lucy stopped speaking then, took a deep breath and swallowed hard.

"How could you know *that*, Lucy?" Evan asked. He could see that she was trembling again. "What is it? Are you sick or something?"

"No, I'm fine," she said in a whisper. "I just need to get out of here." She wiped the edge of her cotton sleeve against her forehead. "It's too hot and dusty today. Let's go back home."

"Home, huh?" Evan sighed loudly under his breath, then started walking forward. "That's easier for you to say than me, I'll bet," he mumbled to himself, not really intending for Lucy to hear. No such luck.

"I *meant* back to the *hotel*," Lucy quickly shot back. He stopped walking and glanced back around. Lucy stood in the road, her head tilted coyly at him. "Okay, McKay. Spill it. What's *your* sad story?"

Instantly, Evan wished he hadn't said anything at all. "There's no story," he grunted.

"Come on," she said. "Tell me. I just know there are some juicy details in there somewhere."

"It's no big deal. I'm just a little sick of this place, too, I guess. You're right—it's way too hot and dusty here."

"Well, I'm not surprised," she replied. "You must be about to expire from the heat in that jacket of yours. Why don't you just take it off?"

Irritated, Evan quickly peeled the jacket off and slung it over his shoulder. He kicked his toe into the dusty ground. He couldn't believe he'd started thinking about home again. The one day that he'd thought was going to be fun had turned out to be a total bust. "Come on," he sighed. "You said you wanted to go back, right? So let's go already."

As they started walking again, Evan could sense Lucy staring at him. He suddenly felt the gentle prod of a finger halfway down his back.

"So where is *your* home, then?" she asked.

Still walking, Evan shrugged his shoulders. "Don't really know anymore," he said. "It's supposed to be Montreal, but it hasn't been that for awhile now. My parents sure don't seem to care, as long as they're as far away from each other as they can get."

"Oh," said Lucy quietly. "I see."

This girl was good, Evan thought. He had to give her credit. She'd managed to turn everything around in a matter of minutes, until *he* was on the defensive. He felt foolish. They walked on in silence for a little while longer, until Evan felt compelled to speak up again.

"So, how about you, then?" he asked. "Your home, I mean. Where is it for you?"

"Well, London, I suppose," she replied. "But I'm hardly ever there anymore, really. Only when school is on. The rest of the time I'm with my uncle, and as you can see, that could be just about *anywhere*. Home is more of a state of mind—for me, anyway—no matter where it is that Uncle Jeff takes us."

"Well, that doesn't sound too bad, if you ask me," Evan remarked. "It's got to be way better than getting stuck in a place where your parents are fighting all the time, eh?"

"I wouldn't know," Lucy replied. "I don't have any parents. They died when I was little."

Evan cringed. Suddenly he felt even more foolish. At least he *had* parents to complain about. "I'm really sorry," he mumbled. "Really."

"It's alright," she shrugged. "You didn't know. The worst thing is that I don't remember that much about them now. Everything is a bit foggy." She fingered the locket around her neck. "I don't like to bother Uncle Jeff too much. I think that it upsets him to talk about them. Sometimes I have these dreams about my mother, though."

Evan didn't know what to say. He chewed on his bottom lip as they walked in silence. He was relieved to see the hotel again, just a few hundred yards ahead.

"Don't give up on your parents," Lucy murmured. "Not just yet, anyway."

"Huh?" Evan grunted. "What do you mean? Why not?"

"Well, I'm not sure about your mother—I've not met her, after all—but your father's certainly not finished with it yet. I can tell, you know. It's right there in his eyes. Clear as anything. He's still very much in love with her."

"How would *you* know?" Evan asked, suddenly feeling uncomfortable. He wished now that he'd never said anything to Lucy about his problems. It was his business alone; private and personal—definitely *not* for public consumption. And now she was jumping all over it, like she had the right to pass comment. Besides, he'd forgotten for a second that he thought *she* was a little crazy.

"It's just a feeling I have," Lucy answered.

A strange chill swept across Evan's flesh. He felt even

more uncomfortable now, and a little embarrassed, too. "A feeling?" he asked. "What? Like getting mental emails from weird little animals?"

Lucy suddenly felt herself turn cold, too. "Wha—what's that supposed to mean?" she stammered. "You don't believe me, do you? Or anything I've been telling you? I thought *you* were different!"

"Well ... you've got to admit it, Lucy, it's kind of creepy—all this animal telepathy stuff. You really can't expect me to—"

"I should have known!" she interrupted, shouting at him now. "I was right about you from the beginning! You don't know anything!"

"Take it easy," Evan whispered. "People are looking over here at us."

"You're rude and you're ignorant!" she continued. "I was only trying to make you feel better—share with you a feeling I had about someone close to you! It's not my fault if you don't appreciate it! And, by the way, you have about as much imagination as a ... a ... wildebeest! They're terribly dull creatures, in case you didn't know, and—"

"Hey!" Evan held his hands up defensively. "You're not exactly something to write home about, either, you know! Like *you're* not spoiled and stuck-up and—"

Lucy pushed her way past him and grabbed onto the hotel's front doorknob.

"Excuse me! I have some things to take care of."

"Like what? Do you have to consult your crystal ball? Get your Ouija board out and make a call, or something?"

"Idiot!" she snapped. "Oh, and if you think you're still coming with me on this trip, you can think again!"

"As if I care!" Evan blurted out. "I never wanted to go in the first place!"

"Oh, that's right! I forgot!" she shrieked. "You don't like *travelling* that much, do you, McKay?"

And then she was gone—in a flash through the door—leaving Evan alone on the crooked stone steps that led into the hotel. Once again, he immediately regretted everything he'd just said. But hearing her talk about his parents that way, especially how his dad might be feeling—as if she knew what was in his mind? And then the way she was trying to make him believe that there was even a shred of hope left for his family? It had pierced him like a thorn in his side.

"Lucy?" Evan mumbled, as he pulled the hotel door open and poked his head inside. "Come on. I'm really sorry. How about that truce again, eh?" But she was already gone. And what was worse, she'd taken Jack Trenton's guidebook with her. How was he going to get it back? He sure didn't feel like asking her for it now. Evan cringed. His father was going to be furious.

Evan slowly pulled his head back out of the doorway, then turned and slumped down onto the stone steps. He didn't feel like facing anyone else right now, certainly not his father. Lowering his head, he stared down at his shoes for awhile. He'd really blown it this time, and just when he'd actually started to look forward to a bit of adventure. Even Lucy was okay—when she wasn't hysterical. When Evan finally looked up again, Francis Darby was coming toward the hotel from the direction of the market. He suddenly stopped walking—as if he'd just seen something of interest—then quickly retraced his steps, sliding down a dark side alley. Intrigued, Evan left the hotel entrance and walked across the street. Stopping at the corner, he slowly glanced down the alley. In the dim light, he could see the shadowy figures of Darby and another man about halfway down. Darby, a hunting knife in one hand, had the much larger man in a convincing head lock.

"We had a special understanding, you and I, right?" Evan heard Darby sneer as he pressed the gleaming silver blade hard against the other man's flesh. "At least, I thought we did."

The other man, his eyes wide with fear, tried to pull away.

"What is it, Mr. Tyrone? Cat got your tongue?" Darby taunted, sliding the knife up and over the man's chin and poking the sharp tip at his bottom lip. "Or should I just take care of that, myself?"

The other man, his eyes flashing even wider, tried to grunt out a response.

"Before you say anything you might regret," Darby interrupted, "let me make a suggestion. You're going to get out of this town. In fact, you're going to get as far away from the Himalayas as you can. Isn't that right?" Darby slipped the knife back under Tyrone's chin and pressed it deep into his neck, stretching the skin even further.

Evan watched the big man nod his head up and down, slowly and carefully.

"That's what I thought," Darby replied. "I don't want to see you around here ever again. That niece of Parnell's already caught sight of you and your bruises and I don't want any loose ends hanging around. I don't want her telling anyone or asking too many questions, either. Do you understand my concerns, Mr. Tyrone?" Darby lifted the knife away from the man's neck. "You're a liability to me right now. Besides that, I can make it worth your while to get out of town."

"How?" the man croaked.

"By not sticking this very sharp knife into your neck!" Darby snapped. "Got it?"

The man nodded vigorously.

"Excellent," Darby replied. "That's the kind of cooperation I like to see." Without warning, he grabbed the man by his bandaged thumb, twisted his arm and twirled him around, pressing the knife up against his spine. Tyrone grimaced in pain.

"Get out of here then," Darby snarled, "before I get carried away. I don't know what it is, Mr. Tyrone, but I can feel my hand twitching ever so slightly." He started to chuckle. "It must have developed a nervous tic with all of the stress I've been under lately. I've been jumpy every since we picked up that mangy beast. This hand of mine might just slip at any moment. It would be a shame for me to have to leave what's left of you to the alley dogs, wouldn't it?"

Darby let go of the man's arm and gave him a final push forward with the toe of his boot. Tyrone never looked up. He just kept stumbling forward, all the way to the far end of the alley and around the corner.

Evan watched as Francis Darby re-sheathed the knife, slid it in his boot top and started walking toward the street again. Evan pressed himself flat against the stone wall of the corner building and held his breath. But Darby shot out of the alleyway, straight past him, and then across the street. He barrelled through the front door of the hotel without looking back. Evan breathed a sigh of relief, waiting for a few moments until he felt safe enough to cross the street and enter the hotel. Lucy would probably be really interested to hear about this, he thought, until he remembered that they weren't speaking.

Feeling miserable, Evan wandered up the stairs and back into his room. He lay down on the small rickety bed and pulled the thin, grey blanket right up to his chin. He thought about his mother's remote cabin in the Laurentians. He had been stuck there all of last March break—six days of endless rain and nothing to do, completely bored out of his mind. Even that, he thought, as he stared at the cracks on the ceiling, would be a much better place to be than the one he found himself in right now.

Dinner that evening was awful. Lucy said no more than five or six words throughout the entire meal, and none of them to Evan. In fact, she refused to look at him at all. As soon as she'd finished eating, even before dessert had been served, she asked to be excused, complaining of a bad headache. Evan endured the rest of the dinner conversation between Sir Jeffrey and his father for as long as he could, eventually asking to be excused, too.

Evan slowly made his way upstairs again, not quite sure whether he was relieved or upset to find the guidebook sitting on the floor outside of his room. He had it back, at least, but leaving it there like that was a clear sign from Lucy that she never wanted to speak to him again. He bent over and scooped it up as he entered his room, tossing it down on the end of the bed. He quickly wiggled out of everything but his undershorts, flinging the rest of his clothes over the back of the small chair in the corner. He picked up the guidebook again and flipped it open to the poem Trenton had copied down all those years ago. He flopped down on the bed and started to read where he'd left off in the bus.

On the night before the dance, Mad Carew seemed in a trance,
And they chafed him as they puffed on their cigars:
But for once he failed to smile, and he sat alone awhile,
Then went out into the night beneath the stars.

He returned before the dawn, with his shirt and tunic torn,
And a gash across his temple dripping red;
He was patched up right away, and he slept through all the day,
And the Colonel's daughter watched beside his bed.

He woke at last and asked if they could send his tunic through;
She brought it, and he thanked her with a nod;
He bade her search the pocket saying "That's from Mad Carew,"
And she found the little green eye of the god.

She unbraided poor Carew in the way that women do,
Though both her eyes were strangely hot and wet;
But she wouldn't take the stone and Mad Carew was left alone
With the jewel that he'd chanced his life to get.

When the ball was at its height, on that still and tropic night,
She thought of him and hurried to his room;
As she crossed the barrack square she could hear the dreamy air
Of a waltz tune softly stealing thro' the gloom.

His door was open wide, with silver moonlight shining
    through,
The place was wet and slipp'ry where she trod;
An ugly knife lay buried in the heart of Mad Carew,
'Twas the "Vengeance of the Little Yellow God."

There's a one-eyed yellow idol to the north of Khatmandu,
There's a little marble cross below the town;
There's a broken-hearted woman tends the grave of Mad
    Carew,
And the Yellow God forever gazes down.

Evan sighed, then closed the book and tossed it down to the bottom of the bed. Feeling chilled now, he pulled the grey blanket up from where he'd left it on the floor, then swung his legs around and curled them sideways. He gave the lumpy pillow a few good thumps with his knuckle, repositioning it several times under his head before he felt comfortable enough to settle down. He dozed on and off for the next hour or two, mulling over the poem while thoughts about obsession—and all the other things Lucy had spoken of—swirled in his head. At one point, he listened to the sound of a brief evening rain shower as it pelted against his windowpane. The last thing he heard was the plaintive howl of a dog in the distance.

He opened his eyes to a pitch black room, an odd sound still ringing in his ears. It only took him a moment to identify the noise: the squeal of a door hinge, directly below his window. Despite being cautioned by the hotel owner to keep his window closed due to the large swarms of bugs that were always flying about, Evan had decided to leave his open just a crack, hoping that the incoming night wind would move the warm, stale air in his room around. He glanced over to the travel clock he had set up on the small table beside him. It was one o'clock in the morning. He slid out of bed and moved over to the window, peering down below. A lone figure was scurrying away from the hotel entrance. It paused for a moment, then quickly spun around, looking up at the line of windows on the second floor before suddenly darting across to the other side of the street. Evan had pulled his head away from the window as soon the figure had turned, but he quickly pressed it back against the rippled pane of glass. He was straining to see now—trying desperately to make out who it might be—but the grey shadows of night continued to obscure his view. The figure stopped just once more, pulling something out from beneath its clothing and laying it gently on the ground. A group of scruffy looking dogs that had been loitering in an alleyway rushed forward into the moonlight and began to eat.

"Lucy?" Evan whispered to himself. "*What* are you up to?"

He felt around in the dark for his clothes and struggled to pull them on again. They felt cold now and he shivered as he finished dressing.

"Stupid girl," he whispered again. "Think you can do this all alone, eh?" He banged his toe against the bed. Limping, he tiptoed toward the door in his socks, holding his breath as he gently turned the knob, praying that the old, rusting hinges would be quiet just this once. "If you ask me, Lucy," he continued, mumbling under his breath, "what you really need is someone to save you from your own crazy imagination."

Suddenly Evan stopped in his tracks. He crept back across the room and retrieved Trenton's guidebook, slipping it once again into the inside pocket of his jacket.

Carrying his shoes under his arm, Evan made his way down the stairs. He held his breath again, trying his best to avoid the old wooden floorboards that he remembered squeaking the loudest. Everything was dark and quiet and still on the main floor. Even Tenzing, who usually manned the reception desk well past midnight, according to Lucy, had already retired to his bed. Evan crept through the lobby and up to the front door. He raised himself onto the tips of his toes and peered through the small glass panel that was set into the wooden door, watching and waiting until the shadowy figure finally disappeared around the street corner.

Evan slipped into his shoes and out into the night. There was a strong smell hanging in the air—older and earthier and more of animals than usual. Streams of moonlight shimmered down into the street where they pooled onto the surfaces of several puddles, still lingering after the early evening cloudburst. Evan leapt over them, trying not to slip on the surrounding mounds of slick mud. He stopped at every street corner, holding back just long enough to make sure Lucy had not detected him.

Before he realized what was happening, Evan had followed her right out of town and onto one of the old hiking trails that cut through the forest. For a place that was generally considered remote, Evan was shocked at the number of human items littering the trail—discarded water bottles, snack bar wrappers, maps and, most distressing, reams of discarded toilet paper. Being out here in the middle of the night was insane, he thought, as he picked his way past the little pockets of mess. But it was too late to turn back now. He had no idea where he was or even how to get back to the hotel.

Despite their steady ascent, Lucy appeared to be picking up the pace. Evan, breaking into a sprint every now and then, was determined not to lose her. Instead of following Lucy to "save her from her own imagination" as he'd originally intended, his pursuit had now turned into an attempt to keep up with her for another reason—his own survival. Lucy seemed to know exactly where she was going. He reached into his jacket lining and pulled the guidebook out. Walking briskly, he flipped through it, letting the light from the moon illuminate the pages as he searched for the map that the sadhu had drawn earlier in the day. His heart sank. The page had been carefully torn out. He quickly flipped forward—to Trenton's map—and was relieved to find that it was still there.

As silently as possible, Evan kept moving, straining to hear the faint crackling of twigs and branches as Lucy made her way through the forest ahead. It became increasingly difficult to catch his breath as each minute passed, then each quarter hour. The steep twists and turns of the terrain were becoming harder to navigate and there was a growing chill in the air. He noticed that the wind seemed to be shifting about, and every now and then the ground at his feet would suddenly darken as the moon disappeared behind a thickening layer of clouds. Evan zipped his jacket up against the wind and prayed that Lucy, at least, had some idea of what she was doing. He didn't have a clue.

10

THE PATH TO ENLIGHTENMENT

AS A STEADY DRIZZLE began to fall, Evan tugged at the strip of Velcro behind his collar, dislodging the thin nylon hood that was rolled up inside. He pulled it out and then over his head. Fearing that the old guidebook was far too unstable to endure even a mild soaking, he unzipped the front of his jacket and squeezed it back into the inside pocket. In the distance, he thought he heard a rumble of thunder. If a storm was coming this way, there was no telling how much more of a drenching he would have to face. Weather around here, he suspected as he looked up at the mass of billowing black clouds hovering above his head, would probably be much more intense than back home. He hoped that Lucy had thought to prepare herself.

They had been travelling for a while before Evan realized that he'd forgotten his watch. He had completely lost track of time. Had they been out on the trail for two hours now, or was it three? He couldn't be sure. The steady drizzle had been increasing at a much more alarming rate in just the last little while and had now turned into a heavy, stinging rain. The sound of the water hitting against the nylon hood of his jacket was making it even harder to hear Lucy's movements through the forest ahead. Evan tried referring to Trenton's map every now and then, though he disliked the idea of exposing it to the elements. He would have to follow a little closer, he finally decided, despite the increased threat of being discovered. He stayed just behind from then on, watching the wide grey flaps of Lucy's coat billowing out with each gust of wind as she wound her way along the trail and through the trees. She tugged at her own collar every now and then, trying to pull it up even higher to shield her face against the driving rain. At one point she even fell clear off the trail with a thud and a muffled shriek. Evan ran forward, peering over the edge to where Lucy was sliding down a muddy embankment on the back of her coat. He considered rushing down to help, but she had already come to an abrupt stop in front of a large boulder, halfway down. She picked herself up, briefly examined the extent of the mud drenching, and then started the steep climb back up, grumbling the entire way.

Evan almost ran right into her soon after that, when she suddenly decided to stop for a rest in a small clearing where a number of old trees had fallen. He grabbed hold of a thick, waist-high tree branch, and spun himself back around, taking cover at the forest edge. At the same time, Lucy flopped down on one of the fallen trunks. She looked up in his direction for a second, as if she'd heard something. Evan held his breath, worried that his tired wheezing might finally give him away. But she turned and looked the other way just before he was forced to exhale. For now, at least, he was still under cover.

The rain had tapered off for the moment and most of the clouds had moved aside. Shafts of moonlight filtered down into the clearing, casting unusual shadows on the forest floor. Evan, pressing his back up against a tree, slowly began filling his lungs with air again, even allowing himself the luxury of closing his tired eyes. A minute or two later, a strange noise forced them open again. No longer resting peacefully on her tree trunk, Lucy was twisting all around—first in one direction, then another—as if she were engaging in some sort of strange ritual dance. Evan watched, totally confused. Seconds later, Lucy's grey coat was lying on the ground and she was still twirling about, emitting all sorts of shouts and squeals and the occasional curse. When her sweater and trousers suddenly landed on top of the coat, too, Evan froze. What was happening to her? A brief flicker of moonlight finally answered his question, illuminating Lucy—distraught and shivering—hopping about in her underclothes. She was cursing loudly now, this time at a number of big, black bumps on her arms and legs. Leeches.

Evan grimaced. The old tree trunk she'd been sitting on must have been crawling with them. She might have even picked a few up on her downward slide through the mud. He felt in his pocket for the tiny box of waterproof matches he always carried with him and absently fingered it. It was a real shame, he thought. Here he was, holding onto something that might help, while Lucy was suffering just a few yards away, covered in slimy, sucking, disgusting leeches.

Evan looked around, noticing that the clearing, like many other spots along the hiking trail, had been turned into a small garbage dump—a place where all sorts of used items had been left behind by the hundreds of hikers passing through. Evan circled around the clearing until he came to a stand of trees directly in front of Lucy. He hesitated, fidgeting with the matchbox again and wondering if he should just come clean and reveal himself right then and there. He tried to imagine how she might react. Not a pretty picture. Instead, he carefully pushed the tree branches to one side and leaned forward, tossing the matchbox onto the little pile of trash nearest to Lucy's writhing form. It landed dead centre with a gentle "plop." Flinching, Evan closed his eyes, afraid of what might come next. When nothing happened, he opened them again. Lucy had stopped her frantic prodding at the leeches and was looking around, trying to determine where the strange sound had just come from. Finally, her eyes fell upon the refuse pile and the little box sitting pristinely on top. Squealing with delight, and forgetting altogether about the sound, she picked the matches up. Shaking with cold, Lucy made several attempts to light them, tossing the ones that refused to co-operate onto the ground with disgust. At last— and with a triumphant cry from Lucy—one burst into a steady flame. Evan watched as she held the match as close to the flesh on her arm as she could stand. She tugged at the leech until the heat forced it to let go. She repeated the process again and again, shuddering with revulsion as the last leech finally let go. She flung it onto the ground with the others and stood rubbing her arms, as if she wasn't quite sure the ordeal was over. She picked up her clothing then, shaking each piece out vigorously before she dressed, probably fearful that other leeches had infested them while she wasn't looking.

With one last, forceful shudder, Lucy slipped her arms into her coat sleeves. But there was something else now, Evan noticed—a sudden flash of movement in the tree nearest to

Lucy. From a spray of leaves hanging just above her head, a shimmering snake—as thick as a garden hose—carefully lowered itself toward her. As it slipped closer, Lucy lifted her hand and absently brushed at her hair. The reptile retreated. A look of casual annoyance crossed her face as she continued to look down, trying to button her coat with her other hand. The snake slipped down again, just touching the crown of her head. Lucy sighed and looked up this time, coming face to face with something that, clearly, she was not expecting. Evan heard her gasp. She froze where she was standing; too terrified to move. Evan was not at all familiar with the types of poisonous snakes in the region, but judging by Lucy's reaction he decided to ask about it later. He bent down, searching in the dark for something to throw. His hand closed around a large rock and when he lifted it up and hurled it through the trees, the sound of it slapping hard against the ground did just what Evan had intended it to. The snake quickly lifted its head back up into the spray of hanging leaves and silently slithered away along the top of a branch.

Lucy suddenly spun around. "Hey!" she shouted. "Who's out there?"

Evan held his breath.

"Think you're so smart, don't you—following me all this way?" she cried. "You can come out now, McKay! I *know* it's you!"

Evan sighed. This was it, then. He stepped out of the bushes and into the moonlight, actually relieved to finally be in the open.

"Hi, Lucy," he mumbled.

"Oh ... thank God. It's really you," she sighed, clutching

her hands together as she fell forward onto her knees. She let out a long breath, as if she'd been holding it in ever since she'd left town.

"I thought you said you *knew* it was me!"

"I didn't completely. Well ... I wasn't totally sure," she replied, looking up. "I guess I was just hoping. It could have been someone a lot worse, right? What are you doing here, anyway, McKay?" she continued, as she stood up and busied herself with brushing debris off her clothes. The sound of relief in her voice had suddenly turned to irritation. "And how did you know where I'd be and which way I was going?"

"The other map?" Evan replied, patting the bulge in his jacket where he'd stashed the guidebook. "The original? Trenton's? Remember?"

"Oh," she replied tersely, clearly annoyed with herself for having allowed such an oversight. "I forgot about that."

"Besides, Lucy," Evan continued, "you've been charging through here like a stampeding elephant. It would have been easy enough to follow you without any map at all."

"Oh, *really?*" she replied, making a sour face. "Well, I can assure you that it isn't necessary to trouble yourself any longer. I've been out in places like this before, you know. I can handle it."

"Like you've been handling all this rain and mud, I guess," Evan replied. "And the leeches, of course. And that big snake just now must have been an interesting distraction for you."

"You've been right behind me, *all* this time?" she asked, her eyes wide open and staring. "Watching me? That's really creepy."

Lucy's mind began to race, trying to remember every

detail of every single thing she had done since leaving the hotel. She grimaced. She must have looked ridiculous slipping down that muddy embankment, then jumping around and squealing as she fumbled to light the matches in the dark. Had he seen her struggling to get out of her clothes? Shivering in her underwear? Lucy swallowed hard. He must have. She could feel her cheeks burning red.

"You okay?" Evan asked.

"I'm fine," Lucy replied brusquely. "Why didn't you come forward and say something instead of skulking around in the dark like that?"

"Well," Evan began, "I figured that the way you were feeling about me right now, you'd just make a big fuss—throw another one of those fits of yours or something. Right before you tried to give me the slip for good."

"You're right about that," Lucy said indignantly, tossing her head back. "I probably would have. Face it, McKay, I *don't* want you here," she snapped. "And I don't need you, either. As you've obviously seen, I'm quite capable of taking care of myself—rainstorms and leeches and snakes included. In fact, I would appreciate it if you left as soon as possible. Go back to town before you get yourself into some real trouble out here. Besides, I've still got a long trek ahead of me. I don't have time to stand around here chatting all night or playing nursemaid to some spoiled city boy. I've come this far without any of your help. See? I can be pretty resourceful when I have to be," she smiled, waving the little box of matches at him. "You just have to know what to look for."

"Spoiled city boy, huh?" Evan replied, smirking. "Okay. Whatever."

"What's that supposed to mean?" A note of nervousness

crept into her voice.

"Who do you think threw those matches into the pile of junk so you could find them?"

Lucy's face was like thunder. "You?" She held the matchbox out in the moonlight and squinted at it, her heart sinking as she read the tiny stamped message on its side: "Manufactured in Canada." The initials "E.M." were scrawled next to that in thin black marker. "Okay, okay, I get the point," she snapped. "Here, you can have these back."

"Well, if you're *sure* you won't be needing them again," he smiled.

Evan caught the matchbox in midair as it flew toward him. Lucy shoved her hands deep in her pockets and stared at the ground. "So what's the deal, anyway, McKay?" she asked, kicking the tip of her shoe against a rock. "I thought you didn't like all this wilderness survival stuff."

"Could you maybe call me Evan first?" he asked. "And then I can tell you the rest."

"Okay, then, *Evan*," she sighed. "What's the deal?"

"Well, not liking something doesn't automatically mean that you can't be good at it, does it?"

"I suppose not," she replied slowly.

"I spent three weeks of the last five summers way up in northern Saskatchewan—before my parents split up, that is." Evan began. "That's where my grandmother's family came from. My dad kind of insisted on it. I guess he thought that if I stuck it out enough times, I'd learn to like it. But tipping a canoe over in freezing cold rapids and portaging through sludge and running away from drooling, snarling bears and swatting mosquitoes the size of birds was never really my idea of fun. It was always the absolute worst three weeks of the year for me—I hated every single second. I did get pretty good at it, though." He stared at Lucy. "But hey, what about you? I would have figured you'd be an old pro at this kind of stuff by now—going off around the world with your uncle, looking for all your cryptoids and stuff."

"*Cryptids*," she sighed.

"Whatever."

"We always have people to help us," Lucy replied. "You know—guides and porters and such."

"Didn't have to do all the dirty work by yourself, right?" Evan asked.

"No. I guess not."

"They even made your tea for you in the morning, didn't they?" he grinned. "Come on, Lucy. Admit it."

"Perhaps," she replied, refusing to look him directly in the eye. "And I imagine that a resourceful person like yourself would know how to make a thing like tea way out here. Am I right?"

"I've had some experience."

Lucy kicked at another rock. "Well, I suppose, in that case, you can stay."

"Stay!" he replied, his eyes widening in disbelief. "Because I can make tea! Are you serious! Who says I want to stay, anyway? I was just following you to make sure you didn't get into any big trouble. I think I've seen enough now to know that it's a lost cause! I'm heading back. And you should be coming with me."

"I certainly am not!" Lucy tossed her head again and glared at him.

"You're hopeless out here, Lucy. I'm serious. Really hopeless. I don't think I should leave you by yourself."

"Then don't."

"So what, then?" he asked, exasperated. "You're refusing to come back with me? Is that what you're doing?"

"No," she replied, staring hard at the ground again. "What I'm *doing*, I believe, is asking you to stay."

Evan groaned. "This is that important to you?"

"Not just to me, Evan!" she cried. "Don't you understand that? This is more important than me! And though I'm sure you'd be happy to stand here and argue with me about it for half an hour, it's more important than you, too! There are too many weird things happening! We have to find out why, and what we can do about it. And whether you believe me or not, I'm convinced more than ever that it all has something to do with here and now and the animal—our animal—and with what Jack Trenton was trying to say in those notes of his, too. The answer is here, right under our noses. I can feel it."

Evan rolled his eyes. "Come on, Lucy! How could it? How could one little animal like that affect every other one on earth and turn everything upside down like this?"

"See?" Lucy replied, throwing up her hands in frustration. "Nothing's really changed, has it? After everything that's been going on, you *still* think I'm crazy!"

"It's not that! It's just that I ..."

She turned quickly on her heels and began marching down the trail. "Go back, McKay! I'll take care of this by myself. Why don't you just go back to the place you feel the safest!" she shouted angrily.

"That's the problem, Lucy!" Evan blurted out. "I don't know where *that* place is anymore!"

Lucy turned and stared back at him.

"You're scared, aren't you?" she asked.

Evan folded his arms across his chest and sighed. He cleared his throat and stared up into the sky.

"Sure I am," he answered quietly. "Aren't you?"

She didn't say anything to him right away. Instead, she slowly walked back up the trail, coming closer and closer until she was merely inches in front of him. Standing on the tips of her toes, she placed her hand on his arm for support.

"Absolutely petrified," she whispered into his ear.

"Well, I'm glad we finally got that straight," he replied, clearing his throat again. "I feel a lot better now. So let's go."

Confused, Lucy pulled away from him. "But I'm not going back, Evan. I can't. I told you that."

"Neither am I, Lucy. But I think we should go now—go on, I mean. And, if it matters at all to you, I don't think you're crazy. Not *that* much, anyway."

"Thanks."

"Don't mention it."

"I don't intend to Evan," she sighed. "Ever again."

11

THE LESSON

"YOU KNOW MORE about stuff around here than I do, Lucy," Evan complained as they continued their trek northward. Hours had passed. The thick forest of the night had finally given way to a different type of landscape. They were crossing the barer foothills now, and the white-capped mountains in the distance loomed closer. "You're going to have to help me out here."

"Oh, really?" she replied, raising her eyebrows and grinning. "I would never have guessed! You come across like such a seasoned traveller, McKay. Anyway, you read the guidebook, didn't you? From cover to cover, you told me."

"Come on, Lucy, okay? Quit teasing," Evan protested. "Fill me in. Please."

Lucy smiled. "Well, since there's no way to send you back now, and we don't want you putting your foot in your mouth and offending anyone, I suppose I could try to fill you in on the finer points of culture and tradition here. At least, as much as I know."

"Where are we going, exactly?"

"Where the 'X' on our little map says to go, of course. I checked it out with a bigger map before I left the hotel. Turns out it's a *gompa*—a Buddhist temple. There's a monastic community there, too—a place of learning."

"Trenton's monastery?"

"Maybe."

"Why are you wearing that white thing around your neck?"

"It's a *khata*," Lucy answered, "a ceremonial silk scarf."

"For ...?"

"You need permission to enter a *gompa* from the lama— the spiritual leader there," Lucy replied. "You put a donation inside the folded scarf and present it to him. He accepts the donation and then either takes the *khata* to keep, or blesses you by placing it back around your neck."

"Oh."

"See those stones that we're about to walk past?" Lucy asked, pointing to a spot not too far ahead on the path, where a large collection of squared rocks, engraved with symbols, had been piled on top of each other. "They're called *mani* walls. They're covered all over in a Tibetan Buddhist inscription that says '*om mani padme hum.*' That means, roughly, 'hail to the jewel in the lotus.' Just remember that it's Buddhist custom to always walk on the left side of those walls. Same with the *chat-dar*, the prayer flags over there." Lucy pointed again, this time indicating a row of tall poles set into the ground, each bearing, from top to bottom, long lengths of material that rippled in the wind. "They're printed with Buddhist Sutras—or prayers—that are 'spoken' when- ever the flags flap around. It's a means of releasing the prayers to the heavens. Flags can be yellow, green, red, white or blue, symbolizing earth, water, fire, wind and space. You have to remember to circle sacred sites and temples in a clockwise direction—that's how people here believe that the earth and the universe revolve. Never step over a person's feet—always walk around them—and never offer anything with your left hand. Only use your right or both hands together—" Lucy glanced up then and suddenly stopped talking. She grabbed Evan by his sleeve. "Looks like we might be here already," she said quietly. She nodded toward a huge building in the distance, looming out through thick bands of mountain mist—a structure of stone and earth, clinging to the side of a sheer cliff wall, illuminated by shafts of morning light. It was balanced there so precariously that Evan couldn't help but imagine that a good, strong wind might be able to topple it.

"Wow," he whispered. "I guess if you were seeking someone who 'lived beyond the clouds,' this would be a good place to start," he said, repeating the words that Lucy claimed the sadhu had spoken.

They journeyed on, making their way across the steep hills toward the monastery, then up a flight of stone steps that led to the front entrance—a huge, brightly coloured door with an ornate gold knocker at the centre and a hanging handle of coloured fabric. Two monks came to greet them, and after noticing Lucy's *khata*, led her and Evan into a small vestibule where they were asked to wait. A few minutes later, the lama entered, and Lucy held the *khata* out to him.

"*Namaste*," she said, folding her hands in prayer and bowing her head.

The lama returned the greeting. He opened the *khata*, removed the donation, then placed the scarf back around

Lucy's neck. He opened another door, this one leading into a large hall, where rows of small candles were burning. Dozens of ornate carvings, decorated in the five colours of the elements, looked down at them from every wooden column and beam.

"Please come in," the lama said, gesturing for them to enter. As they made their way into the hall, Evan noticed that another monk had joined them. He stood silently, just behind the door.

"You have come here to ask something?" the lama inquired. "Perhaps you have an interest in learning of our order?"

"Yes," Lucy replied. "Well, sort of.... We're students, actually."

"Students?"

"We were wondering if you could tell us about some things that we're interested in."

"What things would those be, my child?"

"Um ... things about the natural world, I think."

"You think?" he asked, tilting his head to one side. "Do you not know what it is that you seek?"

Evan shot Lucy a look. Students? The lama wasn't buying it. He fumbled inside his jacket for the diary.

"Look," Evan interrupted, fingering the book as he spoke. "Someone told us to come here. Well, he told her, actually." He glanced over at Lucy with a sheepish smile. She was probably going to kill him for not following her plan.

"A spiritual person?" the lama asked.

"Yes," Evan replied. "A sadhu. He drew a map—a map to this place. But it turns out that there's another map—the same one, actually—in this bo—"

"Where did you get that?" The man standing behind the door moved slowly out of the shadows, his eyes transfixed on the book in Evan's hand. His head was shaven and he wore a maroon and yellow robe, like the other monks, but there was something about him that seemed very different.

"You've seen it before?" Evan asked.

The man nodded. "Yes," he said quietly.

"So it's true, then," Lucy remarked, looking up at Evan. "Trenton did come here all those years ago—right after his encounter with the cryptid on the mountainside." She turned to the monk. "Do you know this man—Jack Trenton?"

"No," he replied softly, shaking his head. "I did not know him." He paused for a moment, looking first at the lama, then at Lucy and finally directly at Evan. "I *am* him."

"You're Jack Trenton?" Evan exclaimed.

"Yes," he replied. "Or I was. That was long ago now, when I belonged to the world outside." He stared again at the book in Evan's hands. "Where did you find this?"

"I didn't find it, actually," Evan explained. "It was given to my father by a man he knows. He let us borrow it when he heard we were coming to Nepal."

"His name was Trenton, too?" he asked, his voice sounding strained.

"Yes."

For the first time, the trace of a smile crossed the man's face. "I can't believe that Roger kept this for all these years," he sighed, taking the book that Evan was now holding out to him. "He is well?"

"Um ... I think so. My father saw him just a few days ago in London."

The man smiled again, then suddenly looked very intently at Evan and Lucy. "You've read the journal entries?" he asked.

They both nodded.

"Then you will understand what I struggled with in those times," he replied. "Balancing the power of what I wanted to do with what I knew I should not. I came to this place seeking guidance and was fortunate to find what I was looking for—an understanding of the intricacies of existence and the sanctity of all life."

The lama, who had been standing to one side, listening quietly, stepped forward then and bowed to Lucy and Evan. "I must go now. But I will send someone back with food. I imagine you have both had a long and tiring journey." He turned to Lucy. "I'm leaving you in very capable hands, my child. I pray that you may find the answers that you seek." He bowed to the other man and left the room.

The man who was Trenton turned to Lucy. "I sense that you are gifted."

"Gifted?"

"You see things that are veiled to others."

"Well ... I ... uh ... sometimes have strong feelings about people and places, or things that might happen."

"Just as it was with someone in your family before you," he replied. "There is a person who comes to you now in dreams. Am I right?"

"My mother," Lucy answered. "But how do you *know* that?"

"It's a natural thing," he said. "You have inherited this gift of yours—this gift of insight—from a soul who came before you. You did not know this about yourself?"

"I wasn't sure," Lucy replied nervously. She hesitated then, pressing her hand against the locket around her neck. "But I do have a lot of dreams about her."

"That is just her way of speaking to you," he replied. "She is guiding you now from another place."

"How can you be sure?" Lucy asked.

"Because I am like you," Trenton replied. "I have similar insights. They have been with me all of my life. A sixth sense, some people call it—both a blessing and a curse."

Lucy shivered. She remembered her uncle using the exact same words.

Trenton looked directly into Lucy's eyes. "In fact, I dreamed that someone like you would be coming here today. That is why I was waiting by the doorway. I was watching as you approached. You were drawn to this place, too," he said, "just as I once was."

"Yes," Lucy replied. "I knew I had to come here, I'm just not sure why."

"You must have many questions," he replied.

Lucy took a deep breath and looked straight at him. "You see, there's an animal ..." she suddenly blurted out, "a very strange animal."

"Strange?" he asked. "In what way?"

"My uncle is a zoologist," Lucy continued, "a cryptozoologist, actually. Sir Jeffrey Parnell. He's been leading a number of expeditions around the world to investigate lost and undiscovered creatures, and some legendary ones, too—like loch monsters, sasquatches and yetis, that sort of thing ..."

The man smiled. "I believe I have had some experience with one of those myself."

"Well, that was *all* it was about," Lucy replied, "at first, anyway. But then this expedition came upon something quite different. It's an animal unlike anything ever encountered before—with scales and feathers and fur and gills. It's like a fish and a reptile, a bird and a mammal—everything! Like all the creatures of the world, all rolled up into one. It has these strange eyes, too. You could be looking into them and then, all of a sudden, they'll begin to glow—bright and smouldering, as if they were burning from within."

Jack Trenton was staring even more intently at her now.

"And I've been having these visions, too," Lucy continued, "thoughts about it that I can't let go of—ever since I touched it and it spoke to me. In my thoughts, I mean." Lucy shot a quick, nervous glance in Evan's direction, and then at Trenton. Surely one of them was about to tell her she was crazy. Evan, however, nodded his encouragement, and Trenton's eyes widened as he spoke.

"As such a thing would be in your nature to experience."

"My uncle doesn't know yet what this creature is, but he's convinced that it's something unique," Lucy continued, less hesitantly now. "He's performed an examination and a number of tests, but the results haven't—"

"Tests?" he interrupted. "The animal was captured?"

"Yes."

"But it is free now? In no one's possession? Correct?"

"No," Lucy replied slowly. "It's in Dhunche—with my uncle and some other men."

"But it should not be," he murmured under his breath, "if ..."

"If what?" Lucy interrupted, suddenly nervous. "Please tell me what it is. I need to know."

"I can only tell you what it might be or, at least, what I think it is. You may have heard this place referred to as the 'abode of the gods'?"

"Yes," she replied.

"I have always believed it is called that with special reason," he continued. "If a state of enlightenment—or heaven, as you may prefer to call it—indeed lies somewhere beyond the clouds, then surely there is no place on earth where one can be as close to it as in this paradise on high. It is breathtaking here, isn't it?"

Lucy and Evan both nodded.

"People have been discovering this for themselves for centuries," he continued. "From ancient times, many who lived here believed that the gods and the goddesses of man made their homes in the shadows of the Himalayas. The people of Nepal call Everest *Sagarmatha*, or Head of the Sky. The Sherpas and Tibetans call the great mountain *Chomolongma*—Mother Goddess of the earth. It is truly a rare thing to find a place where the energy of two great faiths ebb and flow without incident. It is much more than tolerance or understanding; here there is a true sharing of gods. This is a place of great sanctity." Trenton looked at them and smiled. "Now consider this. If man can worship according to *his* own beliefs, then shouldn't the creatures of the natural world—the birds and beasts, insects and fishes—be entitled to the same? To follow a spiritual path, to have saints and angels and prophets—sacred ones of their own?"

Evan shrugged.

"I suppose so," Lucy replied. "If you truly believe that we are all created by the same Divine Being."

"As I feel is so," he replied. "And as many others believe, too. There is still so much that we do not fully comprehend, especially about this truly unique place. But the family of mankind seems not to recognize the sacred nature of these hills, these forests—of all that lives and breaths in this realm. They march through this special world with little thought for anything but their own desires, trampling the delicate saplings beneath their feet, causing the snow on the mountainsides to thunder and fall, fighting each other over tracts of land that belong to no one, trying to take what they can never hope to possess. Sadly, it has been this way for years now." Trenton paused, turning away from Lucy and Evan. He took a few steps toward a nearby table, where the candlelight flickered in time with his movement. He gently held a long wooden match, using it to light a new candle from the flame of another. When he spoke again, his voice was quiet and sad. "But when these people dare to cross that final line, when they finally take that which is truly forbidden, holy to the kingdom of beasts—when the earth's creatures realize that one of their most sacred has been imprisoned, a cry of sadness will echo across the land. There are those who say it will begin with the voice of the jackal. It will sound ..."

"Three times," Lucy whispered.

Trenton gazed at her, his eyes wide with wonder. "You have heard this?"

"Yes, just a few days ago."

"Then what I fear may have already begun," he said. "Many things that cannot be explained will soon come to light."

Lucy wandered over to one of the carved wooden chairs that sat along the wall and slumped down, resting her head in her hands. Looking pale and tired, she slowly nodded. Trenton turned to Evan.

"These things *have* already begun to occur, then? Strange

things, unnatural things? Tell me! It sometimes takes many days for news of the outside world to reach us here."

Evan nodded his head, too, though his eyes, wide and staring, were glued to Lucy. "I'm sorry, Lucy," he murmured. "I'm sorry I didn't believe you before."

Trenton placed his hand on Evan's shoulder. "You must tell me all that you know. Now. Please."

While Lucy listened quietly from the chair, Evan related as many of the strange occurrences as he could remember.

"There is one thing that I have come to understand here," Trenton remarked when Evan had finished. "A synchronistic balance exists in the natural world—a balance that must be preserved. The moon is said to hold the energy of the female; the sun the male. The two must be joined in the heavens and remain so for the universe to function as it was meant to, as it was decreed. And so it must be on earth. Male and female united—two equal halves of one whole; two parts of the same puzzle. The jackal's cry is one of sadness and loss, and that great wail will echo throughout the air and across the land and under the oceans, and it will continue until that which has been taken is restored. It will grow stronger as the days pass, too. More things will occur, I fear, until the world can no longer ignore what is transpiring. It will become impossible for things to go on as they have done before."

"Isn't there anything than can be done?" Evan asked.

"Perhaps," he replied, "if the right person intervenes. But there is no guarantee. If someone of bad intention manages to undo the work of the righteous, then all will be lost. Many believe that our actions on earth determine what we will be in the next life, moving us up or down the chain of existence on our way to enlightenment. This is the path of one's karma; one's destiny. Those who dare to offend the gods and not heed the warnings will drop in their place on this earth like heavy stones, and be forced to begin the long climb back up again. Greed and obsession can be powerful forces. I know, for I have felt the strong pull of temptation in my own life." Trenton turned the old travel guide over in his hands, gently running his fingers over the well-worn spine. "When I touched that creature on the mountainside all those years ago, something powerful flowed through to me. It filled my thoughts day and night until I longed to possess it completely. When I realized that there was nothing else in the world—and no one—who meant as much to me anymore, I became truly terrified. What had I become? My obsessions worried me so deeply that I took flight here, just to find solace." He looked hard at Lucy then. "It might turn out to be the same for you. From what you have told me, this creature of yours may be of an even greater power than mine. There are, after all, many levels of sanctity. Some of these beings— the highest among them—are untouchable. They were never intended to be encountered by mere mortals. I know how these strange feelings move through you. I know how they can make you feel; even one like you, whose heart sincerely strives to be pure. But you can find the strength inside you to resist the temptation—do not doubt that."

Lucy nodded, her eyes heavy with worry. "I have those feelings. I find myself wanting to keep the creature, to be near it every moment," she said. "Even being away from it now is almost unbearable. Am I only going to find peace if I ... I—"

"Come to dwell in a place like this?" he interrupted, shaking his head. "I don't think it is necessarily so. For me, it was the right choice; the only choice. But each of us must find our own path to peace and salvation. But one thing is certain: the animal *must* be returned to the place from which it was taken in order to restore that which has been disturbed. You have the ability to act on this, Lucy. Remember that. Perhaps this is where your salvation lies. The balance I have spoken of is a precarious one—tied to the living, breathing force of the planet. It is a natural power that is everywhere and all around us. The sun must rise in the sky every day, and the moon in all the phases of her eternal cycle must come to us at night. There can be no other way. Male and female—never one without the other. Two halves, one whole."

"I don't understand," Lucy murmured, resting her head in her hands again.

"Perhaps, with faith, you will."

Trenton turned then to Evan.

"You have a part to play in all of this, too," he whispered into his ear.

"Me?" Evan exclaimed. "How?"

"She trusts you," he replied.

"No," Evan sighed. "I don't *think* so ..."

"You may deny it, but it is the truth, nevertheless," he replied, "and you must help her. It will be hard for her to give it up, but the animal must be set free. There will come a time when her feelings will deceive her. She will believe that by following those feelings, she is doing the right thing. But you must not let her give into her longing. Do you understand what I am saying?"

"I think so," Evan replied, hesitating.

"Is there something else?" he asked. "I sense that you have another question."

Evan nodded, pointing to the book. "The poem. Why did you write *that* poem in there?"

"Poem?"

"Here," Evan said, taking the book from Trenton and turning to the page. He handed it back when he'd found the place and waited while the man read.

"I remember it now," he said, smiling. "It was during our long trek through the mountains. One of the Sherpa guides recited it to us around the fire one night, right after we heard the first strange cries and whistles in the distance. He offered it as a sort of omen. Some English fellow he'd led through the mountains once had a habit of reciting it constantly, he explained—a gentleman who vanished without a trace on a later trek. I imagined, at the time, that he was just trying to scare us. I actually found it rather amusing at first and made a point of writing it down. But after my encounter with the beast and all that I experienced afterward, I couldn't help but feel that the poem may have been more prophetic than entertaining. Days later I wrote this note to myself—'Remember this.' It may have been just a poem, but then again, people often say that life imitates art. Perhaps it had a deeper meaning. That Sherpa had offered it as a warning not to intrude upon a world that isn't fully understood. In the days and even years that followed, I began to appreciate his intentions more and more. I realize now that there are things in the world that must be respected, that must not be tampered with."

Trenton walked over to a beautifully carved cabinet that sat along one wall and opened a drawer. He pulled out an old piece of yellow cotton cloth—a paisley-patterned bandana—and walked back to Evan and Lucy. He unfolded it to reveal three strands of thick, silvery grey hair.

"It wasn't lost, then," Evan exclaimed. "You kept it all this time."

"It was as much of it as I could allow myself to keep." He looked at Lucy. "And you must allow yourself no more when the time comes. You should rest a while now, before you begin your journey back," he said. "But not for too long. I imagine that there must be someone, somewhere, wondering about the two of you?"

"An uncle and a father," Lucy replied quietly.

Evan looked at her and grimaced. "And probably doing a lot more than wondering by now. It must be past noon already. It'll be late when we get back. They're going to be really mad at us." He turned to Trenton. "Do you want to keep the book?"

"Yes, that would be ... no, wait. I would like you to take it back to my brother, if you could," he replied. "With one small addition."

He returned the bandana to the cabinet, removing a black pen from the same drawer. He opened the guidebook to the front, where he had recorded his name all those years ago, and began to write a note. "I suppose we all have someone, somewhere, who might be wondering about us." He looked up at them and smiled. "If, of course, we are truly fortunate."

"Do you really believe everything Trenton said?" Evan asked, as they made the trek back to Dhunche. It was very late in the afternoon now. Deep golden light was still playing across the mountaintops, but the surrounding air was growing much colder.

"I'm not sure," Lucy replied, fastening the top button of her coat.

"What did he mean about the two pieces of the puzzle—the sun and moon and all that other stuff?"

Lucy shrugged.

"Do you really think it's, like, an animal *god* or something?" Evan asked. "That's what he meant, right?"

"I think it could be."

"*Really*?"

"Why not?" she replied, gazing up at the mountain peaks that seemed to reach beyond the sky. "In a place as unusual as this, I think I could believe that anything is possible, couldn't you?"

"You know, I've been thinking about that," Evan remarked. "It's kind of funny, isn't it? Funny, as in weird."

"What do you mean?" Lucy asked.

"That poem about Mad Carew and the green eye of the god. Trenton seemed to think it was some sort of a prophecy or something—that it was art imitating life."

"I think he actually said it was life imitating art, Evan."

"Whatever," he sighed. "But it's really only a poem, right?"

"Of course it is," Lucy replied. "So why is it so weird?"

"Well, think about it. The poem was written about a soldier in the British army in India, called Mad Carew, by a man who was also a British soldier, right? Could Carew have been real? I mean, could this poet soldier have actually known him or heard about the strange way he was supposed to have died?"

"What? You think it was all real and that Hayes wrote a poem about it? The story of Mad Carew and his obsession?" Lucy started to smile. "Come on! I don't think so, Evan."

"Well, you might find it interesting to consider something

else. If it was all true and Mad Carew really did steal the green eye and meet his horrible fate the year the poem was written, 1911, it just so happens to be the exact year that another Carew was coming into the world—one now ninety-six-year-old Melville Carew. See? It all fits, Lucy. Maybe it's some kind of weird curse or something."

"That's just silly, Evan," Lucy shot back. "You of all people should know that! In fact, I can't believe you even came up with the whole idea."

Evan shrugged his shoulders. "But I thought you just said that in a place as unusual as this, you could believe that anything's possible? Right?"

Suddenly, Lucy felt the beginnings of an icy shiver run up and down her arms. She slapped at them a few times to get the blood flowing, then pulled the collar of her coat even closer. "I'm really cold, Evan. Let's go home."

Lucy unlocked the door to her room. She was filthy, and more tired than she could ever remember being, but sleep would have to wait. She pulled a rickety chair up to the table where the creature's enclosure rested, and watched him sleep. Although her body was still, her mind refused to stop twisting and turning. She felt guilty about the worry she and Evan had caused her uncle and Mr. McKay. Returning to town just before midnight, they had tried to slip unnoticed through the hotel lobby, only to be intercepted halfway to their rooms by Jeffrey Parnell and Alec McKay. Both were frantic with worry and furious almost beyond words that they had not been told where the two of them were going or when they'd be back. Lucy's hastily invented story about an early morning hike and losing track of time did not fully satisfy either one of the men, but they were so relieved to have them back that the resulting lecture was only mildly distressing.

The creature sighed softly in its sleep before resuming its regular, rhythmic breathing. Lucy started at it, her mind still grappling with all that she had learned at the temple. Could this small animal—so defenceless and unguarded here in her room—really be what Jack Trenton thought it might be? On the one hand, it was hard to imagine—too strange, too unbelievable. On the other, there was no question that this animal was very different. She'd missed him terribly, so much that it had actually ached. It was hard for her to even begin to balance the strong feelings she had now, the overpowering need she felt to protect him from harm, with what she feared she might have to do. But maybe Trenton was wrong. Maybe she wouldn't have to let him go. She brushed those thoughts aside as she considered something she'd momentarily forgotten. Melville Carew was on his way—at least she hoped he still was. If he did manage to arrive soon, Lucy was determined to seek his counsel regarding Francis Darby. Perhaps he might have some helpful insights about the animal, too. Feeling a little more hopeful, Lucy stood up and made her way across the room to her bed. In seconds, she was fast asleep.

12

THE INTRUDERS

BARELY FOUR HOURS LATER, Lucy was awoken by the sound of muffled thumps and loud voices coming from somewhere in the hotel. A dog was barking in the distance. She climbed out of bed and pulled on her robe before creeping toward the door. She stood quietly for a few seconds with her hand resting on the knob, trying to determine what was happening outside. Finally, curiosity overcame her. She pulled the door open and gingerly stepped out onto the landing.

"What the devil's going on down there?" Sir Jeffrey was shouting as he leaned over the stair railing. "What's all the noise, Tenzing? It's four-thirty in the morning!"

"Someone's banging at the door, Mr. Jeffrey!"

"Well, open it, man! They'll have the whole town stirring if they keep that racket up!"

The door to Alec McKay's room discreetly opened a crack, while Evan's door flew wide open.

"What's going on?" he mumbled, stumbling barefoot onto the landing as he tried to fasten the top button of his jeans.

"Is there a Jeffrey Parnell up there?" a gruff voice shouted up the stairs.

"Indeed, sir."

"I've been on some damned gruelling trips in my time, Parnell, but this one beats them all! Roads around here are a mess—potholes the size of craters! Feels like days since we left Boston! I gotta tell you, I'm not real impressed so far!"

"I'll be right there!" Sir Jeffrey shouted down, his voice strained. "Lucy, could you help me to the lobby? I believe our illustrious guest has finally arrived. He doesn't sound terribly happy, I'm afraid."

Lucy reached for her uncle's arm as he slipped off the first step.

"Here, let me give you a hand," Alec offered, as he rushed forward and grabbed Sir Jeffrey by his other elbow.

"Wait up for me, then," said Evan, covering a yawn with his hand.

As they made their way down the stairs, Lucy glanced back, eying the door to Darby's room. How could anyone manage to sleep through all the commotion?

"Bad enough arriving at this hour!" the gruff voice still bellowed from the lobby. "But now this *person* here informs me that the rooms aren't ready! I've told him that I'm Melville Carew, but it doesn't seem to be getting the results it usually does!"

An elderly and very agitated figure stepped out of the shadows. Slightly built and balding, he had tufts of white hair sticking out from behind ears. The pale flesh at his receding hairline was pulled as tight as a drum, revealing a network of pulsing veins. One thick blue one that ran just under the surface, above his right temple, was twitching wildly.

"Umm ... Tenzing," Sir Jeffrey stammered, turning to the

reception desk with his eyes wide and staring. "You knew that Mr. Carew was about to arrive, didn't you?"

"Yes, Mr. Jeffrey," the hotel manager replied, wringing his hands, "but no one said three people coming! Only one room is aired out. But I'll try to fix it fast!"

"Well see to it that you do!" Carew barked back, before he turned to face Sir Jeffrey. "Are you Parnell?"

Sir Jeffrey nodded and extended his hand, only to have it ignored.

"I've got a big bone to pick with you about that car and driver your foundation had waiting for us in Kathmandu!"

"You got a car and driver!" Evan exclaimed, turning to his father with a look of disgust. "How come we had to spend eight hours on a creaky old bus?"

"Evan!" Alec whispered through his teeth. "Drop it!"

"Eight hours on a bus sounds a whole lot better than what we had going on, kid!" Carew shouted out. "Took us *fourteen* hours! And that driver they sent was seventy-five if he was a day. The old duffer kept getting lost—three times at the last count! And that's not to mention the two hours we had to sit around waiting for those yaks to move off the road!" He turned back to the reception desk and growled. "Don't you people have laws around here about having those things penned up?"

Tenzing smiled and shrugged.

"Getting down on the ground in Kathmandu was no picnic either," Carew continued. "Captain Forrester had to circle a dozen times before we could land. Then he had to abort three times thanks to those damned vultures flying all over the place! It's a miracle we weren't killed! I swear those things were deliberately trying to hit us!" The muscles in the old man's face began to quiver as he clenched his jaw in anger.

"Very curious, Mr. Carew," Sir Jeffrey remarked. "Though not unexpected, of course, considering all that's been happening."

"What are you talking about, Parnell?" he snarled.

"You *must* have heard about all the strange things transpiring in the natural world? The odd occurrences?"

Carew sniffed in disgust. "They're calling it the 'Revolt of the Animals.' Seems like the media has to come up with a ridiculous name for every little thing that happens!"

"*Little* thing?" Sir Jeffrey began. "But I hardly think—"

"Speaking of Boston," Alec suddenly interrupted. "We heard something on the radio about an incident at the airport there. When you didn't arrive, we wondered if you'd been delayed ..."

"You bet we were!" Carew shot back. "But no damned lobster's going to stop me!"

"I beg your pardon?" Sir Jeffrey remarked.

"Some jumbo jet's cargo door flew open just as Captain Forrester was being cleared for takeoff," Carew replied brusquely. "Hundreds of crates of lobsters spilled onto the runway—there were thousands of those devils crawling about. We had to wait for hours while they cleared them away. Strange thing though. They didn't scatter off like you'd expect. No, these little beauties lined themselves up on all the runways, neat and tidy, like they were determined to cause a scene. Craziest thing I ever saw! Only good thing about it was when I thought to send someone out to pick a few of them off the tarmac. We shoved 'em in the plane's microwave. Don't taste quite as good as when you drop them in boiling water, but it was miles better than the usual airport catering."

"I'm terribly sorry that your trip wasn't more enjoyable, Mr. Carew," Sir Jeffrey remarked. "Perhaps you'll feel better when you and you're associates have settled into your rooms and had the opportunity to freshen up."

"Associates?" Carew snapped, slowly turning around. "Oh them," he replied flatly, as if he had completely forgotten he wasn't travelling alone.

Two other bedraggled arrivals stood in the front lobby behind Carew: a thin, weedy-looking man in his forties, weighed down with three overnight bags and a large black briefcase, and a much taller, much younger woman clutching a small round hatbox in one hand and a square makeup case in the other.

"This is my personal secretary," Carew snarled. The thin, weedy man shuffled forward, kicking an overnight bag that had slipped off his shoulder along the floor in front of him.

"That had better not be *my* bag, Sedgwick!" Carew snapped.

"No, of course not, sir," the man replied meekly.

"And this lovely creature here," Carew continued, turning to his right, "is my ... um ... travelling companion, Miss Burnaby. Say hello to everyone, Constance."

The young woman smiled very briefly, as if it took a great deal of effort just to move her lips.

"Delighted," Sir Jeffrey crowed, extending his hand again. Constance looked up at him blankly and cracked the gum in her mouth. Flustered, Sir Jeffrey turned away and began to introduce his niece and the McKays.

Lucy had not said a word since entering the lobby, unable to take her eyes off Melville Carew. She was shocked and disappointed with her first impression. She had expected so much more—a man of dignity and distinction, a kindly champion of honourable causes. All she had been able to determine so far was that he was loud and rude and obnoxious. How could she possibly confide her concerns to a person like that? When she finally glanced over at Evan and caught his eye, there was a look of desperation on her face.

"Now that we've finally got those tiresome introductions out of the way, Parnell," Carew scowled, "I want to be updated on the status of the expedition! Immediately!"

"I was hoping we might save that until later in the morning—after a nice breakfast, perhaps," Sir Jeffrey responded nervously. "I imagine we're all rather exhausted right now. I know that I could use some more rest."

The big blue vein on Carew's forehead twitched erratically, and for a moment Lucy worried that he might explode. Suddenly, however, he simmered down and smiled instead, as if he'd just remembered something more important.

"If you insist," he replied, stepping forward and slapping Sir Jeffrey on the back. "And call me Melville, by the way. Please."

"Oh ... well ... alright," Sir Jeffrey responded slowly, taken aback by the sudden change in tone. "That's wonderful ... um ... *Melville*. After breakfast it is, then."

As Tenzing rushed about, moving bags and preparing rooms, the group slowly dispersed, making its way upstairs for a few more hours of sleep. Lucy waited until the room had almost cleared. She walked to the window at the front of the lobby and looked out, amazed that the racket hadn't woken the entire town.

"Not what you expected, huh?" Evan stood beside her, rubbing the sleep from his eyes and looking as exhausted and confused as she felt.

"Not exactly," she sighed. "What now?"

"I don't know," he replied, resting his hand lightly on her shoulder. "Maybe things will look better in the morning."

She nodded, then turned away from the window. As they climbed the staircase to their rooms, an eerie sound echoed through the hotel. It was a jackal, and it howled three times before falling silent.

Dawn hardly had time to break before Lucy heard knocking at her uncle's door, followed by the sound of Melville Carew, apologizing for his abominable behaviour in the middle of the night. It was simply due to the harrowing trip from Kathmandu, he insisted, apologizing again. When Lucy heard Sir Jeffrey reveal to him that an unusual animal had been captured and was in their possession, Carew reacted with surprise and delight. It took all of her uncle's powers of persuasion to convince Carew to eat before knocking on Lucy's door. A short while later, when the two men did arrive in her room, ready to see the animal, Carew appeared almost disappointed. Despite its obviously unique appearance, he seemed to have expected something more, something different. Perhaps it was not a good idea, just yet, Sir Jeffrey whispered into Lucy's ear, to mention anything to Mr. Carew about naming their find after him.

Lucy, growing more protective of her charge as the hours passed, was very concerned at all the extra attention it was having to endure. Even now, with only herself, her uncle and Melville Carew in the room, the creature seemed tense and nervous. It cowered near the back of the enclosure, refusing to come forward, even when Lucy stretched out her now familiar hand. As soon as she could manage it, she politely ushered the two men out of her room and away from the animal's enclosure. Although Carew seemed much calmer and more agreeable than the night before, Lucy was still not sure whether to bring up her concerns about Francis Darby. It appeared, however, that her decision would have to wait. Moments after her uncle excused himself, leaving Lucy alone with Carew for the first time, Darby himself emerged from the shadows, appearing on the landing in front of them. Completely ignoring Lucy, he thrust his hand out toward Melville Carew, staring the old man directly in the eye.

"Mr. Carew, I presume? I'm Francis Darby," he said, firmly gripping the billionaire's hand. "Sir Jeffrey's research assistant. It's an honour to meet you, sir. I've heard a great deal about you and I've seen your picture in the papers so many times that I feel I already know you."

Carew returned the handshake. "Well, I guess it's out of the bag that I'm here now, isn't it?" he said gruffly, keeping one eye fixed on Lucy. "I'd appreciate it, young man, if you'd keep it to yourself. No need for anyone else to know. I like to keep my personal business out of the press as much as possible."

"Yes, sir," Darby replied. "I understand completely."

"Sir Jeffrey tells me that you were the one who discovered that unusual animal in there," Carew continued, nodding toward Lucy's room. "When you have some time to spare, I like to hear all about it. It must have been quite an adventure."

"It just happens that I'm available right now, if you are, sir," Darby replied, suddenly turning his eyes on Lucy.

Although desperate to hear what Darby had to say, Lucy had the strong impression that she was intruding. Reluctantly, she excused herself, leaving the two men alone on the landing. Making her way down the stairs, she glanced at her watch. It was close to feeding time again. She made her way through the lobby toward the kitchen, where she stopped to take another large tin of mangoes out of the hotel pantry.

There were voices coming from behind Francis Darby's door as Lucy climbed the stairs again—muffled, but tinged with anger. She held back for a second or two in the middle of the staircase as Darby's door suddenly swung open. Through the thin space between the wooden spindles, she could see Melville Carew emerge, his face red and contorted.

"I'm very disappointed in you, Francis!" he snapped, turning back to the door. "I went to a lot of trouble and expense to get you in with Parnell—all those certificates and diplomas to arrange, not to mention scuttling the other applicants. It wasn't easy! And now I find out you've been taking stupid chances? Switching that blasted medication of his for sugar pills, for God's sake, just to keep him out of your way?"

Lucy strained her ears, not quite sure what she was hearing.

Darby was grumbling from behind his half-open door. "You were the one who went spouting off on the phone—asking all about his medical condition! I never would have told you about those pills if I thought you'd blow my cover. What were you thinking, old man?" he snarled. "Those Botox injections they keep shooting in your forehead must be freezing some brain cells, too! And I didn't even know you were coming! You couldn't bother to call? No! I had to hear about it second-hand from Parnell and his niece! I was so furious I punched a damned hole in my wall! So what is it? Don't you trust me anymore?"

"Oh, save it!" Carew growled. "It's no wonder I felt I had to come out here and check up on you! Those pills weren't the only thing you've taken chances with! Skulking around in forbidden forests! It's a miracle the authorities aren't breathing down our necks right now! And messing with Tyrone and that Parnell girl—it's a dangerous business, if you ask me."

"What do you care about *them*, anyway! You're here now and so's the thing you've wanted all this time, right?"

"I'm not so sure about that! It isn't exactly what you promised when you called me from Syabrubesi and broke your *big* news! Have you taken a good look at that beast, Francis? Have you?"

"Of course I have! Glowing eyes and everything! Just like you told me to look for! So what's your problem?"

"They're *green*, you idiot! And they're hardly glowing, either! You must have been seeing things!" Carew sneered. "Really, Francis, I expected more of you. I wanted red eyes! Only red! Just like the other time. If you'd bothered to read my journal, you'd understand that! And now I've come all the way out here, just to be disappointed! If it wasn't for my generosity, you'd still be wandering around those filthy dockyards, living off every greasy soup kitchen in Boston. I've treated you like a son, and this is the way you've chosen to repay me!"

"Fine!" Darby grumbled. "Go home then, if you think there's nothing here!"

"Not so fast," Carew snarled back. "I'm not finished yet! I'll need more time with Parnell and the animal—just to find out what makes that ugly thing tick and to be absolutely certain it's not important. But I'll need that old fool's co-operation to do that, won't I? And I'm going to be depending on you to secure it. So don't let me down again. Keep an eye on them—all of them! And I'll be watching you, too. Just remember that! I expect you'll know what to do if any one of them starts to interfere?"

Lucy heard another reply from inside the room—this one

short and abrupt—before Darby's door slammed shut. Grumbling to himself, Carew turned away and stormed down the hall toward his own room.

Feeling as if all the life had suddenly been sucked out of her, Lucy slumped down on the stairs and held her head in her hands. Her once hopeful thoughts had turned to absolute despair. Clearly, Francis Darby wasn't her only problem, and turning to Melville Carew for help had ceased to be an option. They were working together, and had been for quite some time. But on what, and why? Clutching the tin of mangoes in her hand, Lucy wandered back to her room. She sat down on the chair next to the enclosure, closed her eyes and started to cry. A moment later, the sensation of something brushing up against her arm startled her. She opened her eyes and, through her tears, looked down to see that a small lizard hand had slipped through the bars and come to rest on top of her wrist. The creature's eyes were closed, its body rising and falling with each sleeping breath, and this time when his long, green fingers tightened around her wrist, Lucy did not turn away. Letting his thoughts flow freely into hers, she experienced a powerful surge of energy followed by the same vision she'd had earlier—green, leafy treetops and cool, bubbling waterfalls. This time, though, the creature was there too, languishing on a tree branch. But there was something else—something that Lucy had not been expecting to see. Another body perched next to him, its body as strange and unique and lovely as his own. There were two creatures now, bathed in sunlight and surrounded by such an aura of peace and tranquility that it felt to Lucy as if they had been together like that for a thousand years.

A few hours later, the sound of tapping woke Evan from a deep sleep. Still groggy after the night's disturbances, he glanced across to his travel clock, surprised to find that he had slept through breakfast and quite possibly lunch, too. Annoyed, he rolled off the bed and stumbled toward the door.

"Mr. Carew?" Evan heard a voice calling out in the hallway, as the tapping continued. "Um ... I do beg your pardon, sir. I'm very sorry to disturb you again. There's a slight problem."

"What is it Sedgwick?" Carew snarled back. "I was trying to catch up on my journal entries. You know how I hate to be bothered when I'm doing that. If it's about those damned papers, I've already signed them. I pushed them under your door an hour ago. What were they again?"

"Just standard forms, sir," Sedgwick replied nervously, "from your accountant. Something to do with your latest stock sale."

"Well, I really don't see why they couldn't have waited until we got home!"

"Filing deadline, sir. We left in such I rush that I barely had time to shove them into the briefcase."

"Oh, and guess what, Sedgwick?" Carew suddenly snapped. "You packed the wrong reading glasses! I don't even think these damned things are mine! Everything's all blurry when I put them on. For all I know, I could have been signing my life away on those papers! And I'm having a dreadful time with this journal now. I'm practically writing blind."

"Yes ... well ... I'm very sorry about that, sir. I don't know how that could have happened."

"Anyway, what is it that you want now?"

"Well ... it's ... you see ... it's ... um ... it's ... um ..."

"For God's sake man, spit it out!" Carew snarled again. "I

haven't got all day here. I swear, Sedgwick, sometimes you can be as fussy and tiresome as an old woman!"

Holding his breath, Evan opened his door just a crack.

Sedgwick was standing in the hallway, a pained expression on his face.

"Don't get me wrong!" Carew quickly added. "You're as loyal as a golden retriever ..."

"Yes, sir," the man replied, clenching his teeth behind a thin smile and his hands into tight, pudgy little fists behind his back. "Thank you, sir. I'm afraid it's Miss Burnaby."

Melville Carew let out a long, low groan and opened his door wider.

"What's she done *now*?" he sighed, peering onto the landing. "Where is she?"

"Downstairs, sir," Sedgwick replied, "in the front lobby. There appears to be some sort of misunderstanding about the type of accommodation that's been provided, particularly the shared toilet facilities, and there's a question about the quality of the food service, too ... and ..."

Melville Carew rolled his eyes. "No need to explain any further. I think I get the picture. Men like you and I can always rough it, can't we, Sedgwick? But Miss Burnaby is a creature of great sensitivity and high standards. She expects only the best when she travels abroad."

"Yes, of course she does, sir. It's just that the situation is getting somewhat out of hand. There has been some rather rude name calling and, apparently, a number of threats have been made."

"They've *threatened* her, Sedgwick? How dare they?" Carew suddenly pushed his way past, out through the door and onto the landing. "I won't stand for this sort of thing! I won't! My poor, poor Constance!"

"Well, no, sir. Actually, it's Miss Burnaby that's been threatening *them*. Sir Jeffrey Parnell is trying to intervene. I believe the hotelier's wife is quite upset—hysterical, in fact. She's insisting that Miss Burnaby leave the premises immediately. I just thought that you should know, sir. It reminded me of the incident last summer with that gondolier chap in Venice, when Miss Burnaby grabbed that pole right out of his hand and ..."

Melville Carew rolled his eyes again. "Oh, yes ... well, thank you, Sedgwick," he mumbled. "You may go now. I'll take care of this personally."

"Yes, sir, of course." With a look of pure relief on his face, Sedgwick scuttled off down the hall and into his own room.

Evan kept his eye on Carew, standing in the middle of the landing now, as he quickly straightened his collar, refastened the top button of his shirt, then tucked the trailing tails into his trousers. He made his way to the top of the stairs, pulling the sagging straps of his suspenders back across his shoulders. Licking both of his palms, Carew used them to plaster down the unruly tufts of white hair that were poking out from behind his ears.

Evan slipped out of his room and tiptoed down the stairs after him. As he drew closer to the lobby, he could make out Constance Burnaby's shrill voice, piercing the air like the sound of fingernails on a blackboard. She was giving the hotel owner's wife, a jovial and helpful woman, a good dressing down.

"There are no bugs in my hotel!" Mrs. Tenzing was shouting back indignantly. "Only bugs in here must have come in on you, lady!"

There was a cry of outrage from Miss Burnaby. "How dare you speak to me that way!" she shrieked. "How *dare* you!"

"My whole place is spotless!" Mrs. Tenzing continued to protest. "Bathroom, too!"

"You call that *thing* upstairs a *bathroom*?" Constance Burnaby sneered. "When you have to share washroom facilities the size of a broom closet with all those other people, I hardly think anyone is going to be able to do anything remotely resembling *bathing*, are they?"

Evan slipped behind a doorframe in the dining room and peered around at the scene in the lobby. Constance Burnaby stamped one of her high-heeled shoes hard against the floor.

"I can't believe there aren't better places in this good-for-nothing town!" she shrieked again. "Get the manager! I want to speak to him NOW!"

"My husband is out! I told you already! You deal with me!"

"Come, come, now, Miss Burnaby," Sir Jeffrey interrupted. "Please. Let's all just take a deep breath, shall we, and start again. Now, I believe you have a complaint of some sort?"

"Complaint!" she screamed. "Try *complaints*! The place is crawling with bugs, the food is inedible and the towels are all grey and holey! This place is a dump!"

Mrs. Tenzing clutched her chest and muttered some less than pleasant words under her breath.

"It's hardly a *dump*, Miss Burnaby," Sir Jeffrey offered, lowering his voice to a whisper. "I'll grant you, it's not the Hilton, but Tenzing and his good lady here run a very respectable and tidy little establishment. I *really* don't wish to offend these people, Miss Burnaby. They have been extremely kind and generous to my niece and myself. This is a remote part of the world, a place where beggars can't be choosers. I think you are being a touch unreasonable, if I may say so."

"No, you may NOT say so! Not to me!" Constance Burnaby screamed back, stamping her foot again. "Melville was right. You really are an insufferable old windbag!"

"A ... a ... what?" Sir Jeffrey blustered. "I beg your pardon, madam!"

"Constance?" Melville Carew's voice floated across the lobby. "Could I just have a few words in private? Over here?"

Constance Burnaby puckered her lips into a pout and trotted toward him. She whispered into his ear, just loud enough for Evan—still hiding behind the doorframe—to hear.

"Melly," she whined. "These awful people are making me very unhappy. And it's my birthday, too. Remember?"

"How could I forget a thing like that, doll?" The words oozed out of his old mouth like dribbles of honey. "And you know I was so hoping to do something exotic for this year's celebration. But if you're that upset, perhaps you should just head home. Sedgwick will make sure all of your things are packed up and ready to go within the hour. Then we'll phone ahead and tell Captain Forrester to meet you at the airport in Kathmandu. Of course, I won't be able to give you that very special surprise I've been saving ..."

"Tell me what it is!" she pleaded. "If you *really* want me to stay, that is."

Melville Carew smiled slyly. "You'll just have to be patient a tiny bit longer. And then you'll see, I promise. You don't think I'd have brought you all the way here, do you, if I didn't have something really exciting planned?"

"Well, no, of course you wouldn't," she giggled, linking her arm through his. "But tell me what it is *now*, Melville," she asked again, as she leaned over and blew into his ear. "Pleasssse?"

"Oh ... alright, then. If you insist," he replied. "It's very special. Not exactly what I was expecting, mind you, but worth poking around with anyway, I've decided. Sir Jeffrey showed it to me this morning while you were still asleep. It's a most unusual animal ..."

"What!" Constance sniffed, screwing her nose up in disgust. "An *animal*?"

"Not just any animal," Carew cooed, still trying to placate her, "but a weird little thing that's never been encountered by anyone ever before."

"Really?" Constance's eyes began to sparkle as she caressed the mink collar of her quilted silk jacket. "Is it fur-bearing?"

"Well, yes, it is," he replied. "The end of each strand is flecked with a shimmer of gold. And I've been informed that this creature might possess even more fascinating features than first meets the eye, too. Now, I'll be wanting to take a closer look at those parts myself. But you, honey, you can have all the nice furry bits. What do you think? Isn't that exciting?"

Constance nodded her head and smiled.

"I can see you now, my love," Carew crooned, "awash in a sea of gold-flecked fur accessories: things that no woman on earth could possibly ever possess. No one, of course, but you. You'll be the envy of all the Paris fashion houses."

Evan felt sick. He couldn't believe what he was hearing, but he was relieved that Lucy wasn't there with him. He doubted he had the strength to hold her back from lunging out at the two of them. He looked across the room to where Sir Jeffrey stood, still trying to calm Mrs. Tenzing. Thankfully, he hadn't heard either.

"Maybe I'll stay then," Constance sighed. She looked up

and glared at Mrs. Tenzing. "As long as you keep that horrid woman away from me—and right after she's brought me some extra fluffy towels and a bar of soap that doesn't reek of disinfectant!"

"Of course," he replied, taking her hand in his and leading her away from the lobby. Evan, still watching, slipped around another corner and held his breath.

Melville Carew turned back and winked at the hotelier's wife, pulling a hundred dollar bill out of his pocket and waving it in the air. Mrs. Tenzing, clearly insulted, huffed loudly, then folded her arms and marched into the back room.

"I'm very tired, Melly," Constance sighed. "This whole business with that awful woman has completely exhausted me."

"First a catnap, doll," Carew replied, squeezing her hand, "then a nice stroll through town. That's all you need. Then we'll get old Parnell to give you a look-see at that furball upstairs."

"Oooo ... you're so good to me, Melville," she chirped. Then she looked deep into his eyes. "I just can't imagine what on earth I'd do without you."

Melville Carew smiled at her and squeezed her hand again. "If all of the little projects I've been working turn out like I'm hoping, honey, then you'll never, ever, have to worry about that possibility again."

13

The Obsession

LUCY COULD SENSE the excitement in her uncle's voice as she walked toward him through the lobby.

"Where have you been, my dear?"

"I was in my room, giving the animal some more mango. The next thing I remember I was waking up," she replied, yawning and rubbing her eyes. "I guess I must have fallen asleep."

"Not surprising after all the fuss last night," he said, hooking the telephone back onto its cradle. "I've been totally thrown off my sleeping schedule. Anyway, they've just called from the lab in Kathmandu," he told her, leaning on his cane and clutching a wrinkled piece of paper in his hand. "A few of the results are already back and they're quite startling. I'm beginning to wonder if I've written them down incorrectly." He handed the paper to Lucy and shook his head.

Sir Jeffrey hobbled through to the dining room and lowered himself onto one of the old chairs. Evan and his father were already there, busily setting up some spotlights. Evan caught Lucy's eye as she followed her uncle. He was mouthing some words, trying to tell her something. She couldn't make sense of it. Perplexed, Lucy stared at him and shrugged her shoulders.

"Something interesting, Sir Jeffrey?" Alec called out.

"Indeed, Mr. McKay," he replied. "Far more interesting than I expected. I knew we might be in for some surprises just by virtue of the creature's unconventional appearance, of course, but what I discovered in my physical examination, coupled with this information I have just received ..."

"Well?" Lucy asked excitedly. "What is it?"

"For one thing, the composition of the creature's blood cells and its chemical makeup are highly irregular, making it almost impossible to determine its age. Yet I would have to guess, based on my findings, that it is remarkably old. It also appears to be sterile—incapable of propagating—although this is not something that has happened to it. As far as I can determine, it's not the result of a disease or condition of some sort. It appears the animal was created this way."

"But how does it reproduce?" asked Evan's father, clearly confused.

"It's physically unable to."

"What do you mean? It's the only one of its kind?"

"It may well be. Perhaps, for some reason, it outlived its fellow creatures at some point in their history. We are all made up of cellular matter, Mr. McKay—cells that are dying off from the moment we are born into this world. Perhaps, every now and then throughout its life, this *particular* creature discovered a way to regenerate its own cells."

"And now it's the only one left?"

"Possibly. Or, as strange as this may sound, it may actually be the only one that ever was."

"And you're telling us that whatever this thing is it can live *forever*, too?" Evan exclaimed.

"Perhaps not forever," Sir Jeffrey replied, "but at least for a very, very long time. Let's just say that, in terms of how long each of *us* lives and the way that we relate to time, it might as well be forever."

Later that afternoon, Sir Jeffrey agreed to let everyone observe the captured animal again. Lucy looked up nervously as Melville Carew entered her room. With Constance Burnaby hanging onto his arm, he marched right up to the animal's enclosure. Sedgwick, following closely behind, shuffled up to stand next to them. Francis Darby was making his way toward the door, too, but suddenly stopped, remaining in the shadows of the hallway. Lucy was relieved. The poor creature seemed agitated enough, she thought, without having to catch sight of Francis Darby's face again.

"There! What did I tell you?" Carew crowed into Constance's ear. "It's a real eyeful, isn't it? Get a load of that gold-tipped fur coat it's wearing. Just like I promised, right?"

Constance smiled and snuggled closer to him, running her fingers up and down her mink-tipped collar. "Oooo, yes," she trilled. "Some of those feathers are nice, too."

Awake now, the creature paced back and forth, stopping to grab at the bars every few seconds, peering out through a crooked fringe of drooping head feathers. Lucy stepped forward, positioning herself between Constance and the enclosure.

"It needs more room," she said. "It's frightened. If you could just move back a little, please."

Constance Burnaby eyed her disapprovingly. "And who

might you be again, dear?"

"Lucy Parnell," she replied. "We met last night in the lobby."

"And I suppose that you're an expert on this thing?"

"Lucy's been looking after the creature ever since its capture," Sir Jeffrey interjected. "And she's been doing an admirable job, too. It seems to have taken quite a shine to her."

"So you're the babysitter, then," Constance sniffed.

Lucy glared back, opening her mouth to speak.

"Oh, she's much more than that, Miss Burnaby," Sir Jeffrey quickly intervened. "My niece is well-versed in many aspects of zoology. She's an excellent student of the subject."

Constance Burnaby leaned over and whispered—not softly enough—into Melville Carew's ear. "I don't like that girl, Melly, and I don't like the way she's looking at me, either. Get rid of her!"

Lucy bristled and stepped forward.

"Sir Jeffrey," Carew grumbled, clearing his throat. "I need to discuss some things with you in private concerning the status of our little expeditions. It can't all be fun and games, right? We need to talk about funding and budget plans. Don't want to bore the ladies with it." He tipped his head toward the open door, ushering Constance and Sedgwick out, then stared pointedly at Lucy. "You understand, don't you, Lilly?"

"It's Lucy," she replied.

"Of course." Carew smiled at her, gesturing toward the door again.

"But Uncle Jeff," Lucy protested. "I ..."

"It's alright, my dear." Sir Jeffrey looked at her sympathetically. "I'll watch over our patient for you. Perhaps you can go downstairs and see if Mr. McKay and his son need any further assistance."

Lucy left the room, dismayed that she had been sent out and forced to squeeze her way past Francis Darby—who was still lurking in the hallway. She tried pushing past him toward the staircase, but he blocked her way.

"Sss ... sent you away, too, did they, M ... Miss Parnell?" he slurred, his eyes red-rimmed and glassy. "Well, I know all too well how that feelsss." He reached out for her hand, but she quickly pulled it away. "Per ... haps we can commiserate together?"

"Have you been drinking, Mr. Darby?"

"Mmm ... maybe," he replied, reaching out to grab at the banister as he suddenly lost his footing. "What would you care, anyway? You ... you've never cared about me that much, have you, darlin'?"

"What?"

"I saw you on that s ... s ... street corner," Darby hissed at her.

"What?"

"The day your uncle sent you off to the market—just y ... you and that boy—all nice and cozy."

"Boy?"

"Come on, Lucy. He had h ... h ... his arms around you! Evan McKay—your little guest from Canada. Surely you haven't forgotten that already?"

"I don't know what you're talking about," she shot back.

"You could throw me over time and time again, couldn't you?" Darby sneered. "And ne ... never think twice about it. But no ... not him. Why, you'd barely met him and you let him put his hands all over you, di ... didn't you?"

"What are you talking about! You're crazy!"

"I'm crazy now, am I? Well I'm not listening to any of you

people anymore, especially that sour old man in there. Trying to tell me what to do all the time! I don't really ... n ... need him, you know! And I'll mess around with whoever I want to! Starting with you, Miss Parnell!"

Darby lunged forward then, catching Lucy in his arms. He dragged her close into him, pressing his lips against her face. Lucy pushed her hands against his arms and struggled to pull away.

"Let her go!" Evan cried out from the bottom of the stairs.

"Oh mm ... my! What do we have here?" Darby snickered. "It looks like your knight in shining armour has finally arrived, Miss Parnell." He pushed Lucy back against the wall and leaned over the banister. "No wa ... wait! I think it might be a Mountie! Doesn't he look all proud and puffed-up!" Darby giggled. He reached out for Lucy again and pulled her back toward him.

"I said let her go!" Evan repeated, standing halfway up the stairs. "NOW!"

"I'll warn you, boy!" Darby shouted out. "I can fffl ... flatten you like a bug!"

He swung one arm out in front of him and flailed it about. Reaching the top step, Evan grabbed hold of Darby's sleeve and swung him around until he was half dangling over the stairs. When Evan let him go, Darby stumbled awkwardly all the way to the bottom. He groaned as he rubbed the side of his head, then picked himself up and staggered off.

Lucy rushed forward, not sure whether she should throw her arms around Evan or not. She stopped short of doing it, blurting out a hasty "thanks" instead.

"Don't mention it," Evan mumbled.

Lucy suddenly grabbed hold of Evan's arm and pulled him further down the stairs. "I've been thrown out!" she cried. "Out of my *own* room! Can you believe it? I need to talk to you right away!"

"Me, too," Evan began. "I've been looking all over the place for you! Carew and ..."

"I know ... I know!" Lucy interrupted. "I overheard him talking to Darby. They know each other!" She stopped for a moment, waiting for her news to sink in. But Evan simply nodded. "Carew sent him here to watch the expedition. And Darby's done something to Uncle Jeff's pills, too. Carew knew all about the capture—probably before we did. He's come here for a reason, Evan. I'm just not sure what it is." Her eyes suddenly grew wider. "Maybe I *should* have told Uncle Jeff about it all—then and there—right in front of them. You know, flushed them out in the open. Maybe I should have ..."

"Slow down, Lucy," Evan replied, struggling to digest everything he had just learned. "And back up a little. I thought you weren't going to say anything? I thought you were worried about Darby and what he might do to your uncle? If Carew's mixed up with him, too, then ..."

Lucy closed her eyes tight and sighed. "Okay, okay," she said. "You're right. But we have so much more to worry about now. Carew's behaving very oddly around the animal," she said, shuddering. "What if he's planning to do something with it? I think I'd go mad." She opened her eyes and looked at Evan. "What was it you wanted to tell me?"

"Um ..." Evan hesitated. "You know, if you're that upset, maybe we should just go find my dad and tell him ..."

"No," she replied abruptly, "You were right. Not yet." She looked up the staircase. "But I need to get back up there and find out what's happening." She grabbed Evan by the arm again and pulled him up the stairs before he had a chance to protest. They slipped into Sir Jeffrey's room, quietly closing the door behind them.

"I'm sure I heard Carew mention something to Darby about a journal, too," she whispered. "If he has one, I'd love to get a look at it. It might answer a lot of questions about why he's here."

"Well, that sort of brings me to the reason I've been looking all over the place for you," Evan replied. "I have a gift for you."

"As much as I love presents," she sighed. "I'm not sure I'm in the mood for ..."

"Lucy!" Evan replied sternly. "Be quiet for once and listen. You're *really* going to like this one. Trust me and close your eyes."

He took Lucy's hands and placed them around something thin and flat. She quickly opened her eyes again.

"What is it?" she asked, screwing up her nose. "A book?"

"Not just any book. Open it."

Lucy turned the brown leather cover over to reveal the first page and the bold signature of Melville Carew scrawled in pencil across it.

"His journal!" she gasped. "Where did you find it?"

"I didn't actually *find* it," Evan responded. "It was in his room."

She raised her eyebrows at him. "You *stole* it, Evan?"

He shrugged his shoulders.

"I prefer to say borrowed ..."

"Right out from under his nose, too, I'll bet!"

"No! You would have done something like that," Evan shot back. "I'm not *that* insane! I waited until Carew and his creepy girlfriend had gone for a walk."

"Still, that was awfully brave of you, Evan," Lucy replied, "considering that you could have easily been discovered by Sedgwick, or, even worse, by Darby ..."

Evan suddenly turned pale. "Um ... I never thought about that."

"Well, never mind," Lucy responded. "Carew's journal is here with us now, and that's all that matters, right?"

"I guess so."

"So what does it say?" Lucy asked excitedly, flipping through the pages. "Have you read it?"

"Parts," Evan replied, still looking drawn. "I don't think you're going to like what's in there."

"Why?"

"Start here," he said, opening the book up and pointing his finger. "On this page."

"But look at the date at the top—that entry's over two years old!"

"Just read it, Lucy. Okay?"

"August 18th," Lucy whispered out loud. "Lake Champlain, Vermont."

Incredible night! I still can't believe what happened, and even now find myself wondering if it was real. Dropped the crew off at the Burlington docks 7 p.m. Couldn't stand listening to those idiots any longer! Think they know all about sailing an old wooden beauty like The Golden Goose. *But I swear I'm better off doing everything myself! Stars were just coming out. Went down into the cabin to switch on the navigation lights. By the time I got back up to cockpit, the water—black as pitch—was slamming against*

the hull and the wind was howling like a demon. And those
strange feelings were pumping through me again. Even
before I saw that thing rise up through the waves, I knew
that something weird was going to happen. The air was
warm but my skin felt like ice and the hairs on the back of
my neck were sticking straight up. I reckon I was no more
than a few feet away when it broke the surface of the lake.
Suddenly, I found myself staring right into this pair of wild
and glowing eyes—sparkling like two giant red rubies!

It was a huge serpent—a monster of a thing—at least
thirty feet long from head to tail, with two massive humps
along its back. It let out a loud gasp, then reared its ugly
snakehead backward. I'm not sure which one of us was most
surprised—me or the monster! I was petrified, but I threw a
coil of dock line over my shoulder and climbed onto the fore-
deck. I tethered my safety harness to the ship, then swung
my body way out over the water, as close to the creature as I
could dare. I formed a loop at one end of the dock line, and
then, just like a rodeo roper, I swung it over and over above
my head, finally tossing it out into the wind and lassoing
the big thing around its neck. It was a fighter—I'll give it
that much! Thrashed about in the water, straining against
the rope, while I just kept holding on with all my strength.
It let out a shriek then that was so chilling—so blood-curdling
—most men would probably have abandoned the struggle
out of sheer terror alone, but I wasn't about to give up! The
thing pulled itself right down to the waterline again and
again, trying to break free. It gave one last powerful jerk of
its head and a flick of its big tail, and it finally pulled out of
the loop. It lunged beneath the waves and darted away,
leaving a long trail of bubbles and churning water behind

it—but not before I reached down and grabbed onto an inch of its flesh. Its dark hide felt thick in my hand—like an old rubber tire—but warm to the touch. At that moment, I had a feeling of such incredible power that I swear I couldn't speak—I tried like mad but nothing would come out! I couldn't seem to move anything, either. Figured I was having a stroke, but the whole thing couldn't have lasted more than a minute or two from start to finish.

The image of that crazy thing—especially the unearthly red glow that pulsed from its eyes—it's all still there when I close my own eyes, like the memory of it was burned right into my brain! I had a feeling that I'd just touched something really important—intelligent and old; maybe even ageless, like it knew the secret to living forever. Other things came into my head, too—a feeling that the monster had been able to read my mind when I grabbed hold of it. I got a strong sense it didn't like me that much, but I don't care. Can't say that I liked it too much, either! All I know is I can't stop thinking about it now. It must have been my destiny to be on the lake at that exact moment in time. I was meant to see that thing and I'm going to see it again, too, if it's the last thing I do. It has a hidden power—something really big, I'm sure of it! I just have to figure out how I'm going to get it—how I'm going to harness that energy for myself. I'm not sure what to do yet, but I figure that creature must know something. And if I can't make it tell me, I'll find some other way.

Lucy glanced up at Evan for a second. He could tell by the pained expression on her face that Carew's revelations were very distressing to her.

"I'm sorry, Lucy," he said quietly, "I don't know how to say this but ... um ... it actually gets worse."

Lucy nodded her head and sighed, letting her eyes wander across to the next page.

August 25: Boston, Massachusetts

Arrived back home last night. Haven't felt so alive or invigorated in years! Been reading everything I can find—every book, every newspaper article. I want to know everything about "Champ," the "monster" of Lake Champlain, and the handful of people who claimed to have seen it over the centuries, including, in 1609, the great French explorer himself, Samuel de Champlain! And now me! Took the The Golden Goose *out every evening this past week, sailing her back and forth across the lake, trying to run that damn thing down again. No luck. I might have to look into capturing another creature somewhere else; I imagine there are others of its kind on earth. I've never given up on anything in my life before and I'm not about to start now! Besides, those dreams I've been having are coming fast and furious now—more vivid, too. I know it's just a matter of time before they lead me to my goal.*

September 2:

Today I discovered the fascinating world of cryptozoology— the search for lost and hidden life! I have decided to expand my horizons. I am going to collect all the material I can get my hands on about every mythical creature on the planet, from sasquatches and loch monsters to moor beasts and mothmen. Evidently, it's crowded out there, not just with legendary creatures, but with people searching for them, too!

But I'm determined not to let anyone delay my quest. The rest of the teeming masses will just have to get out of my way if something interesting comes by.

Finding one of those beasts has become my newest obsession. The pursuit of this secret life—the harvesting of an otherworldly power that's bounds are as yet unknown—this is my primary mission now! I must zero in on that one thing I need to find again—those red, glowing, pulsating eyes! I saw them so briefly and yet they possess me now, body and soul! If these suspicions of mine are correct—if a source of untapped power really does exist on the planet in the form of living beings, if the secret to eternal life is locked in the gene pool of some legendary monster somewhere— then I will have to tread very carefully.

I have discovered that these "crypto" people are in dire need of funding. There is one of their little group that appears to be quite pliable, from what I have been able to observe: one Jeffrey Parnell—a pompous, dithering egghead—knighted by the Queen for his years of boring service to the Royal Wildlife Trust. He will provide the perfect cover for my master plan. I'll start by sending large sums of money for his expeditions—anonymously, of course—encouraging him to go to the places that I see fit. Then I'll plant a spy right next to the old idiot, too. I'll only reveal myself when Parnell has stalked my prey for me. Then I can move in for the kill!

Lucy stopped reading and looked straight at Evan, her eyes wild with fear.

Evan took her hand in his and they turned the pages over together. "Here," he said, "this entry's from now."

June 20:

Francis called from Syabrubesi. He's found something of interest, though I'm not convinced yet it's what I'm looking for. I told him to give Parnell a call—we're going to need that old fool to examine the thing. I cautioned Francis not to reveal where he found it. Taking chances with the authorities can be risky, as I'm well aware, and I'm not sure he has the stomach for it. I'm worried about this business over Parnell's pills, too. Francis really should be more careful.

I can't get these blasted dreams out of my head! I had another one last night—same as before—towering peaks, valleys of snow and ice, deep canyons, raging rivers. It must be Nepal! Abode of the legendary yeti! I was so certain that the next call from Francis was going to be a great revelation: that they'd found the trail of a snow beast—footprints or clumps of fur from one of those red-eyed devils! But this other creature doesn't sound right at all, with fur and feathers and gills and goodness knows what else. It sounds like a small, insipid little thing. Could my dreams have been wrong, or are they still trying to tell me something, after all? I need to be certain. I don't want to find out how close I really was to glory after the opportunity has slipped from my hands forever! I'm not telling Francis just yet, but I think I will have to go to Nepal and see this beast for myself.

Lucy quietly closed the book and shivered. "I'm frightened, Evan," she said. She turned then and stared at the thin wall that separated her room from her uncle's, as if she couldn't decide whether she wanted to hear what was going on behind it or not. She hesitated for a moment, then taking a deep breath, walked forward and pressed her ear against the wall. Evan went to stand beside her and they both began to listen.

"So what is it, then?" they heard Carew's voice asking. "What do you think we have here, Parnell?"

"We received the results of the DNA and blood sampling from Kathmandu this afternoon," Sir Jeffrey explained. "There are some inconsistencies. More than I had expected to find, actually. It's quite amazing."

"Really?" said Carew, sounding more intrigued. "Well, what do you know?"

Evan could feel Lucy stiffen up beside him. "Don't tell him!" she whispered under her breath. "Please, Uncle Jeff! Don't tell him anything else!"

"I suppose I'd better take a closer look at this thing then, shouldn't I?" Carew crowed.

"Not *too* close, please, Melville," Sir Jeffrey implored. "He seems a little agitated right now."

"Come on, you miserable thing," Carew was saying. "Are you hiding something from me? You really can't. I'll find out somehow. I have ways, you know."

"What on earth are you doing, Melville?" Sir Jeffrey exclaimed. "Let go of the creature's arm! I think you might be hurting it! The skin is quite delicate there!"

"Relax, Parnell. I'm just getting to know him a bit better. Yes," Carew hissed, "I can see it in my mind again. Just like before! I believe you're right Parnell—he's quite unique, isn't he?" he continued. "But there's something else about you, isn't there, my little friend? I know all about your kind. You're different—a special one—and you're just trying to trick me now with those insipid green eyes. But I won't be fooled. In fact, I think you're more powerful than all the others, aren't you? All those glowing, red-eyed cryptids—the sasquatches and the yetis and the sea monsters—they can't hold a candle to you, can they? They're well below you on the chain of command, I reckon. No better than servants. Do they bow down to you, my friend?"

"Enough of this, Melville!" Sir Jeffrey suddenly shouted. "You're pinching it now! Let go of it at once!"

The animal let out a low, throaty growl. Lucy bristled and began moving toward the door. Evan tapped her on the shoulder and shook his head.

"Hah! I knew it!" Carew shouted back. "Did you see that strange glow in its eyes just now? I was right! The rotten little beast was just trying to trick me! Trying to throw me off! But I'm too clever for it! In fact, I'm too clever for all of you!"

"MISTER *Carew*!" Sir Jeffrey shouted angrily. "I must insist!"

"Back off, Parnell! I've seen inside the soul of one of these things before. I know all about it. It was just a matter of time before I caught up to one again! But I never expected that I would find something extra special this time—the granddaddy of them all! Hey—take your hands off me, Parnell! Let go of me!"

The sound of the door creaking open travelled through the wall, followed by heavy footsteps across the floor.

"Are you done with it yet, old man?" a voice snapped.

"Francis!" Carew replied. "Thank goodness you're here! Get this idiot off me!"

In the room next door, Lucy flashed her eyes at Evan.

"Give me the beast first!" Darby scowled. "You owe that much to me! I can probably get a pretty decent price for it on the black market—it's weird enough to attract attention." He paused for a moment, then let out a soft chuckle. "Maybe some-one will stuff its stupid feathered head and hang it on a wall."

Lucy gasped, feeling herself go cold. Evan grabbed her hand.

"I don't owe you *anything*, Francis!" Carew snarled. "Let's be clear about that! Besides, I've decided to keep it for myself. It's turned out to be of some interest to me, after all."

"So I was right about it?" Darby snapped back. "It is something important, then! And you treated me like a worthless dog! I've worked damned hard for you, old man!"

"For *him*!" Sir Jeffrey exclaimed. "Well, Mr. Darby, I've suspected for a while now that something wasn't quite right with you, but I never imagined that such deceit was going on right under my ..."

"Oh, put a sock in it, Parnell!" Carew barked. "And as for you, Francis, you've been careless once too often! Strutting around, playing the big man, forgetting what you're really here for."

The creature started to growl even louder then, rattling the sides of the cage. Lucy could imagine it pacing faster and faster, growing more and more agitated by the commotion around it. If it hadn't been for Evan—grasping her hand tightly now—she would have burst into the next room long before now.

"I really think we should all just try to calm down." Sir Jeffrey's voice was shaky, but Lucy could tell that he was trying to remain in control. She just hoped it wasn't too late.

"I couldn't agree more, Parnell," Carew replied. "If I'm not mistaken, this thing possesses some kind of secret to immortality. That's what you've really discovered, isn't it? That's the bottom line. It can regenerate itself somehow—

live far beyond the lifespan of anything we know about. I'm right, aren't I? Just think of the possibilities—and all right within our grasp. If we can study this thing and figure out what makes it tick ... dissect it if we have to."

"NO!" Lucy cried out in a pained whisper, staggering away from the wall and toward the door. "He can't do that! He wouldn't!"

"Steady, Lucy!" Evan whispered back. He rushed forward and put his hand firmly on her shoulder. "Just wait! Listen!"

"I really think this outrageous kind of talk has gone far enough!" they heard Sir Jeffrey shout.

"I hardly think you're in a position to comment on what I should or shouldn't do, Parnell. This is my expedition, after all. Bought and paid for."

"But the animal isn't faring well!" Sir Jeffrey protested. "Surely you can see that. It's more agitated than ever—stressed and terrified. I'm afraid I can't provide whatever it may need to survive here. I think that we should ..."

"Then do something about it, man!" Carew snapped back. "You're the expert! Fix it up! Keep it alive! And if you can't manage that, we'll have to think of something else, won't we?"

"And just what did you have in mind?"

"Simple!" Carew snarled. "Clone the thing! Take whatever you need from it to make more of the little beasts—you can get the DNA from it right now. Then if it croaks, it won't matter. We'll have lots of time to experiment with the new ones!"

"That's not a good idea," Sir Jeffrey replied firmly. "In fact, I was just about to suggest that we return it to where it came from, and as soon as possible, too. I have no doubt that

Mr. Darby here can tell us exactly where that might be. There are other ways to observe newly discovered species. We can do it in the wild—the way I prefer to work. Let the animal live its life in peace without human intervention and then document what we see. It's been done many times before by other scientists, to great acclaim and scientific advancement—Dian Fossey with mountain gorillas, Jane Goodall and her chimpanzees, Birute Galdikas and orangutans. We can even name it after you if you want—call it the 'carew.' A creature of the earth named after you—just imagine! Now there's real immortality for you!"

"Fool!" Carew snapped. "That's ridiculous! Stop wasting my time with this simpering nonsense, Parnell! I want the creature cloned!"

"There's no means to harvest DNA here," Sir Jeffrey continued to protest. "That's certainly not my area of expertise and I hardly think we have the time to get anyone here on short notice. Cloning is a highly complicated process. I don't imagine the animal will survive having a sample taken from it now ..."

"Well, I don't much care if the miserable thing dies," Carew snarled, "as long as I get what I need before it does. And if you don't co-operate with me, Parnell, I'll just have to pull the plug on these little expeditions forever. You'll be a laughingstock. You don't have a choice."

"We always have choices," Sir Jeffrey quietly replied. "Some of us, it appears, just keep making the wrong ones."

"Clone it!"

"No."

"Then I'll do it myself if I have to!" Carew shrieked. "I'll get the DNA from it while its body's still warm and take it to someone who knows what they're doing. I'm not some pathetic bleeding heart like you, Parnell. I'm a realist. What would most people want if they had to choose: the salvation of one mangy animal or a chance at immortality? I know what I want. And I'm going to have it, too! Once I've discovered the secret and put it in a bottle, I'll patent it and sell it to anyone who can slap down enough money to buy it—a thousand bucks a bottle! Now that's something I'd gladly lend my name to! We'll call it 'Carew's Elixir of Youth!' Yes! In fact, now that I think of it, I believe that the more of them we can clone, the better. I'm going to need a really big supply source. I'll even consider cutting you in for some of the profits, Parnell, if you do what I ask. You'll be filthy rich! Just like me!"

"I'm not interested." Sir Jeffrey's voice was quiet now.

"Don't be a liar on top of a fool, Parnell! *Everyone's* interested in making a fortune," he snickered. "It's just human nature."

"Not mine."

Lucy felt a sense of pride welling in her. "Let me go, Evan," she whispered. She tried to pull her hand away. "Please. I need to go to him."

Evan shook his head again. "What about Darby?" he whispered back. "He doesn't know we're here. You could be risking everything going in there right now. Let your uncle handle things."

Sighing, Lucy lowered her head and nodded as Carew's voice filtered through the wall again.

"So, tell me what you really came here for then, Parnell. I'm curious. If it wasn't for money, then it must have been for the glory of it—the chance to beat out all the other cryptozoologists. Your name in the headlines, maybe? Or a medal from the Queen? Or better yet, an international honour of some sort? Come on now, be honest about it, at least. Or would you have me believe that you really do harbour some idiotic pipedream about preserving a bunch of stupid, useless animals? Surely you're not that much of an idiot!" He paused. "Or are you?"

"I would hardly call them useless," Sir Jeffrey replied sharply. "We're not the only living beings on this planet. The world is a delicately balanced environment, forever teetering on the edge of disaster. Look for yourself, man! Look what's been happening all around us in just the past week! Something's gone wrong out there and we *all* stand to suffer for it. I firmly believe that it's our duty, as citizens of the world, to try to understand and respect the intricacies of the natural world and preserve as much of it as we ..."

"Save your lecture," Carew snapped. "It's survival of the fittest—always has been, always will be. That's the way I see things. And you're just living in a dream world if you believe anything else. That's the way history will remember you, Parnell—as a pathetic dreamer. Not like they'll remember me! I'm a winner. I play hard, and I play to win!"

"You're not the man I was hoping you'd be," Sir Jeffrey sighed. "That man would have been dedicated to the preservation of living things, not to their extermination, and certainly not for his own gains."

Carew laughed. "You must be kidding! Or you're a bigger fool than I thought, Parnell. I was never that man. Not even close. My biggest concern has always been me and me alone. At the moment I'm concerned about the animal, too—my animal —and all the wonderful little things it's been busy storing up inside. I understand you don't need a very big specimen for

DNA," he sneered. "Something as small as an eyeball would do, especially if it's nice and warm and fresh!"

"What in blazes do you think you're doing!" Sir Jeffrey suddenly cried out.

The metal bars of the cage were rattling wildly now, the creature hissing and squealing.

"Let go of it!" Sir Jeffrey shouted again. "Put down that knife! Have you gone completely mad?"

"I can't just stand around like this any more!" Lucy blurted out tearfully, finally pulling free of Evan's grip. "I don't care about Darby!"

All at once, the creature let out a frantic, high-pitched scream—a sound so blood-curdling and unearthly it shook the walls of the hotel. Lucy answered it with a sharp little cry of her own, then, staggering backward toward the door, reached behind her to feel for the doorknob. Evan rushed forward, frantically trying to block her exit. But she just stopped short and stared up at him, her wet eyes pained and pleading, until they suddenly rolled backward and flicked white. Evan reached forward just in time to catch her as she fainted in his arms.

14

THE ESCAPE

LUCY SLOWLY OPENED her eyes and looked around. She was on the floor of her uncle's room. Evan's face, strained with worry, was floating directly above her. She lifted one hand toward the left side of her head and began to rub it—trying to ease the throbbing pain in her eye.

"What happened ...?" she murmured.

"You passed out." Evan spoke softly, gently helping her into an upright position and then onto the bed.

The frightening sounds next door had stopped. All was quiet through the wall. Lucy sat motionless at the edge of the bed, fighting off a thick feeling of nausea.

"Where did everyone go?" she whispered.

"Downstairs," Evan replied. "I heard my dad yelling out. He came running up when the animal started screeching. That was just before you fainted. I think Darby must have slipped out of the room during all of the commotion. He came back a few minutes later with a bunch of other people—his workers, I guess."

"And Uncle Jeff?"

"They took him and my dad away. Carew gave orders to gather everyone in the lobby. He was still going crazy the whole time, too—screaming like a madman about being a breath away from immortality and how he wasn't going to let anyone ruin it for him. He seemed pretty pleased with Darby, though, said he'd 'redeemed' himself. Then he told your uncle they'd be bringing him back later so he could prepare a tissue sample for transport. Carew's planning to take a piece of the animal to London—to hand over to some cloning experts."

"A piece of it?" Lucy shuddered then looked at the wall. "So he's alone in there? They just left him all alone?" She rose to her feet. The room started spinning. Evan rushed forward and steadied her. He could feel her shaking against him.

"You should sit."

Rubbing at her eye again, Lucy flinched. "No," she said. "There's no time. I have to see him before they come back."

"But I'm not sure if there's much left to see," Evan sighed, then hesitated. "It didn't sound too good in there."

"What do you mean?" she replied, her voice trembling. "Is he ...?"

"I don't know," Evan whispered back, lowering his head. "But I do know that Darby's looking for us. We're 'loose ends' to him, Lucy. And if he catches us, there'll be no helping anyone else."

Bracing herself against the wall, Lucy started inching toward the door. "I'm going in there anyway, Evan. I have to."

Lucy pulled the cage door open and slowly pushed her hand inside, resting it gently against the creature's back.

"It's not moving at all," she gasped, quickly pulling her

hand back out. "I can't feel it breathing, either!"

"Here, let me try," Evan whispered. He pushed his hand inside and prodded the animal with the end of one finger.

"See? It's dead, isn't it?" Lucy cried out. "There's blood everywhere and look—its eye's all mangled! It feels so cold, too!" She buried her face in her hands. "He's killed it!"

"No wait," Evan replied, pushing his hand further down the cage. "It's still a little warm." He rested the palm of his hand against the creature, slowly moving it down the length of its back, all the way to its tail. "I can feel it now, too—real soft—like its vibrating or something. Here, I'll show you." Evan took Lucy's hand in his and rested it on top of the creature. "See?"

Lucy nodded her head. "It's purring," she replied. "It could be trying to heal itself." She began stroking the creature rhythmically then, back and forth along its body, trying to keep time with the shallow puffs of air leaving its mouth.

"Well, that was close," Evan remarked softly, "considering it's the only one of its kind."

"No, it's not," Lucy murmured.

"What do you mean?" Evan exclaimed. "There's another one?"

Lucy, still stroking the creature's back, didn't answer.

"Come on, Lucy," Evan sighed. "Tell me. Did you dream something, or what?"

"I felt it more." She looked down. "From him."

"Does your uncle know?"

"No one knows," she replied. "Except for me. And now you."

"It's the two pieces of the puzzle, isn't it?" Evan said. "Just like Trenton said."

Lucy nodded. "He needs her, Evan. He can't survive otherwise." She took a deep breath and finally turned to face him.

"I know what you're going to say, but please listen to me first. We've got to get him away from here now. Take him back to where he belongs, before anyone finds out."

"I know."

"What?"

"I said, I know."

"You'll go?" she replied, with surprise. "You will? Really?"

"Yes."

Lucy turned to him again, her face anguished and pale. "But we'll be leaving them here," she said. "Uncle Jeff and your father ..."

"They'll be okay, Lucy. I don't think Carew's all that interested in *them*." Evan looked down at the animal. "This is what he really wants, right? Come on. We'd better get going."

Slipping into his own room, Evan rifled through his luggage, shoving a handful of chocolate bars and three small bottles of water into his pockets before he returned to Lucy. She had unfolded an old blanket that was lying at the end of her bed and pulled the cage door open. She grimaced as it squealed against her hand, then reached inside and gently pulled the creature toward her, cradling him in her arms as she carefully wound the blanket around him.

"There's only one problem with this plan, Lucy."

"What's that?"

"We have no idea where to take him—do we?"

Lucy stared ahead and sighed. "Well, I have a general idea, I think, based on where Darby and his men must have been at the time of the capture, and the visions I've been having," she replied. "I have a feeling we should be heading a lot deeper into the forest, right into the middle of the Langtang valley."

"Where?"

"It's an area within the national parkland that spreads north and west from here. We're actually sitting just within the boundaries of the whole park right now, at its eastern edge. It's supposed to be protected; it was designated as conservation land way back in the mid-seventies, I think. The government set thousands of acres of land aside then, for all kinds of animals and plants and birdlife. Dhunche is actually the first checkpoint for the park's entrance, though Syabrubesi is generally considered the trailhead for treks into the valley. But I have a feeling we're going to have to travel a lot further than that to get him back home."

"Is this place uninhabited?"

"No, there are people living there, too, but only a few thousand. They're mainly Tamangs, an ancient Nepalese race of farmers and cattle breeders—very religious. What they practice was originally related to Bon and the pre-Buddhist doctrines of Tibet, but those have been merged now with newer teachings, I think. The old ways and beliefs are probably still circulating, though."

"With strong connections to the natural world?" Evan asked. "To trees and animals and birds and ..."

"Yes."

"Sounds like the perfect place then, doesn't it?" Evan replied, fiddling with the window latch. "Deep into the valley it is then."

"Well, that's *my* guess, anyway," she replied, looking down at the small animal in her arms. "Failing that, we may just have to rely on him. We're taking him home, after all.

Maybe he'll figure out some way to let us know when we actually get there." She looked up at Evan again and made a face. "What on earth are you doing?"

"I may have forgotten to mention the other problem with our plan. Right now, the lobby is filled with people we don't want to bump into. We're going to have to leave through the window."

"Are you joking?"

"Don't have to worry about the animal." Evan gestured to the bundle in Lucy's arms. "He's used to living high up in the trees, right?"

"I wasn't worrying about him," she said, grimacing. "You go first."

The sweet, earthy scent of living things was all around. The Creature suddenly thrust his nose out of the blanket and cautiously sniffed the air. He had been drifting in and out of sleep until then, hoping he might awaken just once to find that the fear and pain had finally gone. Intrigued by what he detected now, he tried inhaling long and deep, filling his lungs. He knew this place! It was their place. Excitement welled up inside of him, spilling out into each limb, spreading through to the clawed ends of his long, lizard fingers. Even the feathers at the top of his head began to quiver with anticipation. His good eye—the one he had hardly dared open since the vicious assault on the other—was beginning to sparkle. He tried blinking it open and shut as the shimmering green fire inside slowly start to stir. Cautiously, he let out a few little squeaks, then a few more. A sudden and rapid barrage of much louder squeals followed as he pushed his arms and legs against Lucy's side, struggling desperately to see past the layers of material encasing him. He wanted to see out. He wanted to be sure.

"What's going on in there?" Evan asked, peering nervously over Lucy's shoulder. "What's he doing?"

"I don't know," she answered. Her voice was trembling as she tried repeatedly to twist the end of the blanket back around the creature's arms and legs. "He's really pushing hard. I didn't think he was *that* strong." She looked up at Evan, her eyes filled with worry. "He might hurt himself if he doesn't stop struggling. You've got to help me calm him down."

Evan stopped and looked around. They had been trekking through the night and his body was tired and aching. It was well past dawn now. He scanned his eyes skyward to where the thick canopy of trees was almost blocking out the sun. Only a few streams of bright light had filtered through, creating dappled shadows on the forest floor. It was serene here, he thought—calm and dark and secluded.

"You know, I think we might be close," he announced quietly. "We must be, Lucy. Just look at him! He's going nuts! We should let him go right here. He knows where he is."

Lucy shook her head. "I'm not sure this is such a good idea."

"What?" Evan exclaimed, staring at her in utter disbelief. "Isn't this what you wanted? Isn't it why we've brought him here? Look around, Lucy! This is just like the place you've been seeing in your mind, right? The one you told me about. And now *he's* telling both of us that this is it—this is where he belongs. I'm sure of it."

Lucy didn't reply. She looked down at the ground instead, pulling the struggling animal even closer.

Evan's heart sank as Jack Trenton's words echoed ove
and over in his mind. "There will come a time when her feel
ings will deceive her," he had said, "but you must not let he
give in to her longing." Evan took a deep breath and reache
over. He tried to gently pry the animal out of her arms, bu
Lucy stood her ground, refusing to let go.

"Come on, Lucy! What are you doing?"

"I'm not leaving him here like this, Evan. I can't!"

"You shouldn't think like that, Lucy." Evan rested hi
hand on her shoulder, trying to provide what little comfor
he could. "It's wrong."

"Wrong? How can you say that?" she cried out, twistin
away. "You know what Carew will do with it if he captures i
again! He's already had a go once! And if it isn't him, then i
will be someone just as bad!"

"But now you want to keep him," Evan replied, as gentl
as he could. "That's the point, isn't it?"

"No! It's different for me! I'm not like that!"

"I know! But you want to keep him just the same, don'
you?" Evan asked, more firmly this time. "Tell me the truth.

Lucy hesitated. "Well ... yes," she replied. "Of course
want to. I want to keep him from all the cruel and horribl
people in the world, people like Melville Carew. I can tak
him somewhere where he'll never be found. Is that so bad?"

"Yes it *is*!" Evan exclaimed. "You'll be keeping him fror
his real life—the one he's supposed to be living. You, of a
people, should know that. You were led to the monastery
Lucy. You were meant to hear the message there, meant t
honour what you'd learned. There's a special place for thi
animal, a place where he belongs. He has a role to fulfil o
the earth, too—a sacred one that you and I can't even begi

to understand. You're the one who taught me this, Lucy! If what you've been saying all along is true, then these strange things that have been going on in the world will just keep on happening, probably getting worse, too, if we don't take him back home."

"I don't care."

"Yes, you do. You just can't see it clearly any more. He has a mate, remember? The other half of him. Think about that, instead. Apart from everything else that's been going on, there's another one out there that needs him—a being that's depending on him. And that's not you, Lucy." Evan put his hand on her arm. "He has a life of *his* own. You've got to give him up now."

"But what about *that*?" she exclaimed, glancing down at the bloodied socket where the creature's left eye had been. "He'll never be the same again."

"It's already started healing a little. You can see for yourself, Lucy."

"But his sight there is gone forever. He'll never be able to see properly with just one eye. How will he survive on his own?"

"He's *not* alone. We already know that. The other one will help him. You're just making excuses now."

Lucy sighed, wiping her tears away with the back of her hand. She couldn't look at Evan anymore.

"I'm right," he said. "You know I am."

Lucy held the struggling animal closer for a second, then dropped her head and sighed again, slowly nodding.

"Let him go, then," Evan said.

"I can't."

"Then give him to me, Lucy. I'll do it for you."

She hesitated for a moment, then suddenly thrust th
wiggling bundle toward him. When he took it from her, Luc
turned and quickly stepped away, stopping by the side of th
trail.

Walking forward, Evan gently peeled the edges of th
blanket back. The creature gripped the sides of the materi:
with his fingertips and pulled his body up, all the while starin
at Evan, locking two wide green eyes on his—smoulderin
and emerald bright. Evan paused and turned his head
Glancing at Lucy, he fought a strange and unexpected urge t
walk back to her.

His excitement mounting, the creature began franticall
twisting his head back and forth, squeaking and squealin
even louder than before. Lucy tried covering her ears, as if
might help drown out her sorrow.

"Wow! Look at him go!" She could still hear Evan
words, followed by a distant rustling in the tops of the tree
She desperately wanted to turn back and look, but somethin
was keeping her feet frozen solid to the ground. She couldn
move or turn her head. Evan came up behind her and put hi
hands on her shoulders.

"He's gone," he said. "The little guy flew right into th
trees—fast as the wind! It was really something. I wish yo
could have seen him. It would have made you feel better."

"But *you* saw him, Evan," she replied, her voice shakin
"And that's enough." She turned to face him then, lookin
down at the empty blanket in his hands. Three strands c
gold-tipped fur lay against the worn fabric. She picked the
up and gently closed her hand around them.

"As much of him as I can keep, right?" she murmure
Evan nodded. She threw her arms around his waist an

pressed the side of her face against his jacket. "I really want to go home now," she whispered.

"Yeah," Evan answered. "Me, too."

As Lucy and Evan turned and walked away, the excited squeals of the creature echoed in the distance, answered by the chatter of forest birds. Soon a different call altogether reached their ears—a sweet, blissful trilling, the unmistakable sound of another's joy.

15

THE RECKONING

CONSIDERING ALL THAT had transpired, the trek back was relatively uneventful. It was very late into the night now, well over twenty-four hours since they had first set out. Drained and exhausted and down to their last quarter bottle of water and half a chocolate bar, Lucy and Evan decided to stop and rest for a while before making the final push for Dhunche.

They found a small clearing by the side of the trail where a cluster of maple trees stood, bathed in moonlight. Evan slowly slid his back down the trunk of one old tree and crossed his legs in the dirt. Lucy, much more conscious of her surroundings after her encounter with the leeches, ran her hands back and forth over a patch of moss at the trunk's base several times before she felt confident enough to settle there.

Evan reached into his pocket and pulled out a mangled piece of foil.

"Chocolate?"

Lucy shook her head.

"Sure?" he asked again. Lucy didn't respond. Evan

shrugged his shoulders. He unwrapped the square of chocolate and popped it in his mouth.

"You okay now?" he asked.

She glanced up at him and nodded, but Evan could still see a trace of sadness in her eyes.

"He'll be alright, Lucy," he murmured to her. "He's back where he belongs."

"I know," she sighed. "You're right. It's just—" Her words were interrupted by a high-pitched scream in the distance—a human scream. Lucy stiffened. "What was that?" The stillness around them had been shattered—the air was suddenly alive with sound.

Evan jumped up, straining to make sense of the panicked screams and shouts that were echoing through the forest.

"Something's happening!" He began to sprint toward the noise, slowly at first and then faster and faster, as the shouting grew more intense. His heart was pounding now. He was sure he could hear his father's voice.

"Evan!" Lucy cried out, struggling to keep up. "Wait!"

Less than a minute later she had caught up to him. He was standing at the edge of a clump of bushes, one hand resting on a branch. He turned and motioned for her to be quiet.

The scene that greeted them as they peered through the brush was one of utter confusion. It was an encampment, half-erected, with tents and supplies and boxes strewn about in no particular order. Only one tent was fully assembled. It stood at the centre of the little clearing, and it seemed to be the focus of everyone's attention. Flashlight beams were spinning out from it in every direction, and Constance Burnaby, sobbing uncontrollably, was crouching on the ground nearby.

"Melville! Melville!" she was wailing, over and over again, holding her head in her hands.

A trio of porters had wrestled someone to the ground. Alec McKay, pressing his knee into the man's back, was trying to tie his hands together with a piece of rope. Sir Jeffrey Parnell, sitting in a large travelling sling, his bandaged foot stretched out in the mud, was shouting something from the sidelines. Relieved to see her uncle alive, Lucy started to move out of the shadows. Evan quickly grabbed her by the arm and pulled her back toward him. Straining to hear the conversation, he lifted a finger up to his lips. "Wait," he whispered, "at least until we're sure we know what's going on."

"But, Uncle Jeff ..."

"He's looks fine! Just wait, okay?"

"Tie him up, Mr. McKay!" Sir Jeffrey shouted, appearing to have taken charge in spite of his condition. "Don't let him get away!"

The struggling man twisted his head sideways and screamed out in anger. The light from a propane lantern on the ground illuminated his face. Lucy gasped. It was Francis Darby.

"What are you idiots doing?" he shouted. "It wasn't me! I didn't do it!"

"But it's *your* knife, Mr. Darby!" Sir Jeffrey shouted back. "We've all seen that dreadful thing before—sticking out of your boot top!"

"It was someone else! It must have been. That knife's been missing for hours," he screamed. "Stolen out of my boot while we were resting back there! I swear it. I didn't tell anyone because ..."

"Someone *else*, Mr. Darby?" Sir Jeffrey asked. "Who? We

were all here, well within sight of each other. And it was you, I recall now, who'd left us momentarily—some story about scouting something out, wasn't it?"

"I heard a noise! I went to take a look!"

"Strange how none of the rest of us heard it!" Sir Jeffrey remarked. "You had plenty of time to slip into Mr. Carew's tent when our backs were turned."

"That was *my* tent, you idiots!" he screamed. "The one I always use! The old fool must have crawled into it and drifted off on *my* cot while I was gone! He just couldn't wait for his own to be put up! *I* was supposed to be in there! Someone was trying to kill *me*! Can't you all see that?"

"Someone mistook Melville Carew for *you*?" Sir Jeffrey asked, laughing in spite of the situation. "And then, without making absolutely sure, proceeded to plunge *your* knife into him? Save your theories and explanations, Mr. Darby. I'm sure the porter will be back with the authorities in a few hours."

Lucy grabbed Evan by the arm. "Carew's dead?" she whispered. "Murdered?"

"Looks that way," Evan replied.

"But why? Who?"

Evan tipped his head toward the man, struggling on the ground. "They seem to think it was Darby there, although he's certainly not making any confessions."

"There," Alec tied one final knot and stood. "That should hold him until the police arrive." He glanced at the tent. "Umm ... what should we do with the uh ..."

Sedgwick, shaking from head to toe, suddenly emerged from the tent.

"Straight through the heart," he announced solemnly.

His voice trembled as he wiped his blood-stained hands with a handkerchief. "He probably died instantly. I've removed the knife and covered him up."

"*Removed* the knife?" Sir Jeffrey asked with surprise. "Isn't that tampering with evidence? Perhaps you should have left everything just as it was ..."

"I couldn't leave him like that, could I?" Sedgwick interrupted. "With that horrible knife sticking up out of him?"

"But any fingerprints on the weapon will be smudged over now!" Sir Jeffrey continued. "I don't imagine the authorities will be able to obtain any useful information from it—certainly nothing that would hold up in a court of law."

"Well, they'll just have to convict Mr. Darby without benefit of his fingerprints then!" Sedgwick shouted back. "Circumstantial evidence will have to do. The murder weapon was *his* knife, after all. And he was here, right at the murder scene. And we were all here, too, weren't we? Witnesses of sorts! We all know who did this!"

"It wasn't me, you FOOLS!" Darby shrieked, struggling against the ropes that were binding him, his face twisted with rage and frustration. "I told you, someone must have been trying to kill ME!"

"What made you do it, Darby?" Sedgwick growled at him. "Greed? A pathetic robbery attempt gone bad? You just couldn't stand to see that dear old man with so much, could you? He told me he didn't trust you anymore."

"Me?" Darby screamed back at him. "What about you? I bet you've been waiting for years to get your hands on that paranoid old buzzard. Paid you a pittance and treated you like a dog, too, didn't he?"

"He certainly did NOT!" Sedgwick replied indignantly,

clenching his fists. "Mr. Carew was a warm and caring employer and I'm proud to have been his loyal and faithful servant all these many ... long ... long years."

"LIAR!" Darby screamed.

Sedgwick lunged forward as Evan's father stepped in to block him. "Let me go, Mr. McKay!" he shouted, flailing his arms about, left and right. "Call *me* a liar, will he? Let me at him!"

"Gentlemen! Gentlemen! Please!" Sir Jeffrey interjected. "We should leave all of this to the police! It's not up to us to hold court here." He glared across at Francis Darby. "If Mr. Darby is indeed found responsible, then I'm sure he will be spending a very long time in prison for what he has done. Justice will prevail in the end."

"You bumbling bunch of morons!" Darby mumbled out of the side of his mouth, his cheek resting flat in the dirt. "You've got the WRONG man!"

"Do you think they *do*?" Lucy whispered to Evan in the bushes. "Could it really be someone else?"

Evan glanced up, his eyes resting first on Darby, then on Sedgwick and Constance Burnaby, huddled together now near the tent. "Who knows?" he shrugged.

Evan moved his foot then, snapping a tree branch in half. He winced. Darby, closest to them, lifted his head toward the bushes, scanning his eyes back and forth nervously.

"Tyrone!" they heard him whisper under his breath.

Evan stepped sideways, cursing under his breath at the broken piece of wood near his foot.

"I guess we'd better give it up now," he mumbled to Lucy. "Anyway, by the looks of it, my dad and your uncle have things pretty much under control."

He took her hand and they slowly emerged from the bushes together, shielding their eyes from the glare of the flashlights that had now settled directly on them.

"Lucy!" Sir Jeffrey exclaimed, struggling with his cane to stand up. "Thank goodness you're all right! I've been worried sick!"

Alec McKay ran forward and threw his arms around Evan. "You okay, son?" he asked.

"Yeah, dad, we're fine," Evan replied, shrugging off the embrace. "Are *you* okay?"

"We are *now*," Sir Jeffrey replied, clearly excited that he had someone else to share his ordeal with. "Though there were some moments earlier when I honestly wondered if your father and I were ever going to make it back to civilization alive. We were dragged out here against our will. Even in my delicate condition, Mr. Carew insisted I be brought along. I imagine he thought that I might be able to find the two of you and that creature again." He looked plaintively at his niece. "Just look at me in this ridiculous travelling contraption, Lucy. The porters have done their best carrying me, I'm sure, but the constant bumping has set my foot off throbbing again. And we've been terribly worried about the hotel staff. We were forced to leave them behind, under guard by one of Mr. Darby's henchmen and ..."

"But you're alright now?" Lucy interrupted.

"Yes, yes," he replied, "more or less, I suppose. And I'm relieved to report that the tables have apparently turned in our favour—not, however, without a most distressing development. There has been a murder. Mr. Carew is dead."

"We know," Evan replied, gesturing toward the bushes. "We were listening to everything from over there."

There was a sudden flurry of movement from Darby, still lying tied up on the ground.

"Check those ropes again, Mr. McKay," Sir Jeffrey shouted out. "We can't allow our prime suspect to escape!"

Lucy took Evan by the hand then and pulled him away.

"You were right," she said, almost whispering under her breath.

"What?" Evan replied.

"You were right," she repeated, a little louder this time. "*An ugly knife lay buried in the heart of Mad Carew.* Remember?"

Evan stared ahead, an icy cold tingle slowly spreading through his body. He turned to her and raised his eyebrows. "Lucy!" he whispered back. "It's what Trenton was saying— the 'art imitating life' thing? Or do you think maybe it's the other way around?"

"I guess sometimes it's *both*," she replied.

Evan opened his mouth to speak, then hesitated. "I can't remember now. What was the next line again?"

"*'Twas the 'Vengeance of the Little Yellow God.'* Although in this case, I think it might be more like justice."

Sir Jeffrey suddenly glanced over.

"What of our little animal, Lucy?" he called out, looking up at them with weary eyes. "What happened to him? We just assumed you took him, but in all the turmoil here, I didn't even ask if ..."

"He's fine, sir," Evan interrupted, "but gone. We set him free."

"I suppose, under the circumstances, that may be the best thing for him," Sir Jeffrey replied with a sigh. "Well away from Melville Carew's unsavoury interests and now this terrible murder business, too. But when everything is back to normal, we can have another crack at finding him again, can't we?"

Evan smiled blankly at Sir Jeffrey and slowly nodded his head before turning to Lucy.

"Of course, Uncle Jeff," Lucy said, nodding along with Evan. As Jeffrey Parnell turned his attention back to the tent and the chaos that lay within, however, Lucy stole a quick glance at Evan. "It will never happen," she whispered. "Not as long as I live."

The low afternoon sun was just starting to fade away into dusk. Evan peered through the small airplane window as Kathmandu gradually disappeared before his eyes. A thick cloud of pollution enveloped the city, and as the Royal Nepal Airlines pilot pulled his craft further away from the ground, Evan could see pockets of smog colliding with the clean, natural mist of the surrounding peaks. The Himalayas shot skyward from there, looming like stark, silent sentinels on the horizon; a stern-looking barrier that only the very brave— or the very foolish—would ever dream of challenging. Leaving had been harder than Evan expected. The plane banked to the left, giving Evan one last look at the city he had fought so hard against visiting. And yet, in the end, he had seen and done so many things here that he could never have imagined, not in his wildest dreams. His only consolation was that he would be back one day soon. The details hadn't been finalized yet, but Sir Jeffrey was determined to continue working in the area, hopefully to locate the strange animal once again. This time, however, he would do things his own way—observing and documenting his find in the wild, away from laboratories and tests and other people's ambitions.

And best of all, for Evan, he'd already asked Alec McKay to do the photographic work that would supplement his research.

Despite Sir Jeffrey's high hopes, Evan was pretty sure that he would never find *that* particular animal again. He wasn't sure how, but Evan knew in his heart that Lucy would never allow it to happen. But maybe, somewhere on his travels, Jeffrey Parnell might have the great fortune of stumbling upon that tiny, undiscovered tree frog—the one he had been searching for all of his life. He could introduce it to the world, save it from extinction, and name it after anyone he chose.

Evan smiled to himself. Although he still considered himself a reluctant traveller, that was one trip he was really looking forward to. In fact, he wouldn't miss it for the world. Lucy would be there, after all. His mind drifted back to just a few hours earlier, when they had said their goodbyes.

"There's something I've been wanting to ask you," Evan had said as he closed the clasps on his suitcase. "Is it a habit of people like you to keep journals or diaries, or something? Of all the significant things in their lives?"

"People like me?" Lucy sat cross-legged on the bed, watching him gather his things into a neat little pile by the door.

"You know ... gifted people—like Trenton said at the monastery—that sixth sense thing. It was *his* journal that started this whole thing, right? Melville Carew had one, too." He'd looked straight into her eyes then and grinned. "So what about it, Lucy? Do your have one of those things or not?"

"Actually, I do." A faint blush coloured Lucy's cheeks as she reached up and tucked a loose strand of hair behind her ear.

"*Really*?" Evan smiled a sly smile. "Um ... am *I* in it anywhere?"

"You could be, I suppose," she'd said, smiling back. "Most definitely."

And that had been all Evan had needed to hear. His thoughts turned back to Jack Trenton. He'd been right, after all. Some things were things worth fighting for, were worth the risk. He turned to the seat next to him, to the place where his father had been dozing fitfully just moments before. But Alec McKay was awake now and sitting up, the plastic meal tray pulled down in front of him. There was a piece of paper and a pen in front of him, too. He looked up at his son and smiled.

"Can't seem to settle," he said, "so I thought I might write your mother a letter."

"Wouldn't it be a lot easier just to call her once we get back?" Evan said, trying hard to conceal his excitement.

"No, no, this is much better," his father replied nervously. "It's been a while since we've had anything much to say to each other. Sometimes you just have to test the waters with these things first."

Evan looked out the aircraft window again, trying to hide the smile that was spreading across his face. The sunlight was slowly fading beyond the curve of the horizon. Darkness would soon be upon them as they raced over the crystal stillness of the mountain peaks below—across northern India and the Middle East, across the countries of central Europe; on and on, past France and over the English Channel to London. And then, maybe—just maybe—all the way back home.

Constance Burnaby arrived at the graveyard by taxicab, her black lace gloves grasping a big spray of colourful flowers. She buried her nose in them for a second or two and breathed deeply, as if the thick, cloying scent could protect her from whatever unpleasant odours might be lingering in such a place. She wasn't familiar with the etiquette involved in these matters, but it seemed that she should pay *some* sort of respectful homage to the man who had just bequeathed her fifty billion dollars—whether he'd known about it or not.

Constance carefully bent down, trying not to get too close to the mound of fresh, moist earth, and tossed the flowers out in front of her. When she stood up again, she was overwhelmed by a strange sensation. She shivered and pulled her fox fur jacket tighter around her shoulders. She was sure that she had heard something—a small, pitiful and strangely familiar voice calling her name. It was so faint and feeble, however, that it seemed to be coming from the ground near her feet.

"Melly? Honey? ... Is ... is ... that *you*?" Her voice trembled in a thin, dry whisper.

All at once, Constance started to giggle. This was just plain silly! She had seen him herself that morning, hadn't she? Lying very still in that red velvet-lined coffin and looking remarkably good thanks to all the makeup and hair gel they'd plastered on him. Nevertheless, he was as dead as a doorknob.

Constance shivered again as she glanced around. It must have been the distant screech of an owl, or the moan of the alpine wind as it whistled down from the mountains. There was no one else here, after all, and nothing at her feet but the last leeches of the fading summer rains. She looked down and grimaced. One of the slimy little devils was trying to attach itself to the pointy tip of her right shoe. She gave her foot a vigorous shake but the leech refused to let go. Shuddering with revulsion, she leaned over, finally managing to prize the thing off with the metal clasp of her Gucci handbag. The leech plopped onto the ground and lay still for a moment before it rallied itself and started creeping back toward her. Fearing that her alligator shoes had already sustained irreparable mud damage, she decided that it was probably time to leave. Constance Burnaby took one last look at Melville Carew's final resting place and sighed. Perhaps he had found peace— that karma thing that the holy men here were always talking about. A man as important as Melville Carew was probably enjoying the fruits of his labours on earth in some other form already, just like the gods promised. Maybe this time he was destined to return as a powerful world leader, she considered, a man of even greater prestige and distinction than before. Fair reward indeed for the life that he had lived.

"Connie?" A voice shouted out from behind her. "Are you coming, muffin? Captain Forrester won't hold the jet past four o'clock." She turned to look at the taxi, idling on the dirt road that ran through the cemetery. Sedgwick—dear, sweet, devious Sedgwick—was waving his pudgy little fingers at her through a thin crack in one of the rear windows. She sighed. He was no Melville Carew, that was for sure, and if it hadn't been for him, she might one day have taken home the whole hundred-billion-dollar estate instead of half that amount. But then again, she probably couldn't have done it without him. Sedgwick, after all, had taken care of all that pesky paperwork. Somehow, he'd convinced Carew to sign over his will, just before he'd swept her into his arms and declared his undying love! After that, he'd been obliged to offer her at least half of his new fortune. It had all worked out rather well, she had to admit. Yes, Sedgwick had definitely proven to be useful. Now, she just had to figure out how to get rid of him.

Constance began to quietly hum to herself. Apart from calming her nerves, it seemed to be an effective means of blocking out the strange little voice that was still calling to her from somewhere near her feet. As she turned to walk back to the waiting taxi, she gave the persistent leech one last boot into the bushes with the toe of her alligator pump. It was going to be next to impossible to get the dirt out of the leather grain now, she feared. But even as she picked her way very carefully through the dizzying maze of mud puddles, Constance began to smile again. The strange little voice had finally stopped, and she knew that if she turned on enough of that irresistible charm she'd be able to convince big, burly Captain Forrester to make an unscheduled stopover in Paris. She had just remembered an absolutely exquisite little shoe salon just a few blocks away from the Champs Elysées....

Gasping for air, Lucy sat up on the bed like a bolt. She shuddered and shook her head, trying to clear away the last remnants of a very strange dream. Her eyes quickly searched the room, but there were no flickering light bulbs here—no sinister shapes on the wall, no Francis Darby lurking in the shadows. Bathed in the golden half-light of Kathmandu's setting sun, her room at the Everest Hotel was considerably more luxurious than the accommodations they'd left behind in Dhunche. When her eyes finally came to rest on her bags by the door, all packed and ready to go, Lucy sighed with relief. She would be home by tomorrow. She rested her head on the clean, crisp pillow again, trying to concentrate her mind this time on more appealing subjects than Constance

Burnaby and Melville Carew and the last leeches of summer.

Things in the rest of the world were finally returning to normal. Word of Melville Carew's death had hit the newswires the day after his body was discovered in the tent. All other stories—including the bizarre happenings in the natural world—had been wiped off the front pages by the billion-aire's passing. In the days since, Lucy had scanned the papers closely, and had even tried to coax the old transistor back into service. Nothing. Just this morning, however, she had heard a small piece on BBC World Service. According to the reporter, it appeared that the animal aberrations had finally ceased. The experts, who had been so clueless as to why these things had been occurring in the first place, had just as little to offer in terms of reasonable explanations now. Lucy had smiled as she turned off the radio to continue packing. She knew exactly why they had stopped and so did Evan.

She glanced at the clock radio by the bedside—still an hour to go before their ride to the airport. She closed her eyes again and smiled, as visions of Evan, already on *his* way home, slowly drifted into her thoughts.

EPILOGUE

DEEP WITHIN the cool, dark sanctuary of the Langtang forest, a small animal with an unusual gleam in one eye scrambled up through the high branches, took his place beside his mate, and handed her a walnut. The few rays of sunlight that had managed to filter down through the thick umbrella of treetops glistened against the golden strands of his coat and the shimmering, iridescent skin on his hands and feet. Feathers of blue and turquoise, scarlet and purple sprouted straight up from the top of his head, then cascaded down his back in a brilliant flash of colour. The feelings of panic and despair that burdened him for days were slowly dissolving. His memories of the Strange Ones—the beings that had displayed to him both the greatest cruelty as well as the greatest kindness— were fading fast. The only reminder of his experience was a faint throbbing sensation at one side of his face, and even though his vision there had turned as black as the night, the Creature was so relieved to be home that it was hard for him to feel anything but glorious elation.

Chirping blissfully, his companion shuffled sideways

along the branch and nestled her body as close to him as she could, until they were wedged together like two pieces of a puzzle. He could feel her warmth radiating through him. Gazing down through the trees to where the river waters danced and bubbled across the rocks, the Creature sensed that the order of the universe was once again as it should be. He popped a piece of sweet walnut into his mouth and felt at peace.

Acknowledgements

FROM THE MOMENT I first read (at age nine) zoologist Gerald Durrell's wonderfully poignant and very funny chronicle of his boyhood on the island of Corfu—*My Family and Other Animals*—I was hooked not only on wildlife conservation and reading, but on the discovery that it might actually be possible for a person to follow more than just one muse in a lifetime. *Carew* has grown out of a love for and fascination with the animal world that I have harboured ever since, along with a conviction that our planet is probably hiding more mysteries and wonders than we could ever hope to discover or understand.

I am continually amazed at the number of creatures that we read about on the newswires and in science journals—many just during the months I was working on this manuscript. Some were brand new, never before seen; while others, long believed extinct, were emerging once again; everything from monkeys and bears to butterflies, birds, frogs and fish. They were found inhabiting the deepest realms of the Coral Sea, a remote island in Indonesia, the swamps of Arkansas, or—as in one recent case (and to my delight)—a dark, leafy forest in the shadow of Mt. Everest! Who knows what amazing things are waiting to be revealed. And yet—sadly—all these marvellous discoveries don't even begin to add up against the number of living things that routinely disappear off the face of the earth forever (with little fanfare), or suddenly find themselves teetering precariously on the brink of extinction.

I would like to thank all of my family—especially Rob and Sam—for their love and support (as always) while I worked on this project. And since *Carew* marks the publication of my seventh book with Key Porter, I would also like to acknowledge everyone there with whom I've had the pleasure of working over the past dozen or so years—along with a very special thanks to my editor, Linda Pruessen, for her constant encouragement, keen insight, wonderful sense of humour and consummate professionalism.

—J.C.M.